The
Glory
ASHES

D1334057

9112000035058 4

THE GLORY GARDENS SERIES
(in suggested reading order)

Glory in the Cup
Bound for Glory
The Big Test
World Cup Fever
League of Champions
Blaze of Glory
Down the Wicket
The Glory Ashes

The Glory ASHES

BOB CATTELL

Illustrations by
David Kearney

RED FOX

BRENT LIBRARIES

KIN

91120000350584

Askews & Holts	01-Dec-2017
JF	£6.99

*h and Tony Lewis for checking
uckworth-Lewis method in
d nine*

09 940904 5

ldren's Publishers UK
ndon W5 5SA

House Group Ltd
ey Auckland
roughout the world

ell 2001
Illustrations © David Kearney 2001

Score sheets reproduced with kind permission of David Thomas
© Thomas Scorebooks 1985

19 20 18

This book is sold subject to the condition that it shall not,
by way of trade or otherwise, be lent, resold, hired out, or
otherwise circulated without the publisher's prior consent in any
form of binding or cover other than that in which it is published
and without a similar condition including this condition being
imposed on the subsequent purchaser.

The rights of Bob Cattell and David Kearney to be identified as the
author and illustrator of this work have been asserted by them in
accordance with the Copyright, Designs and Patents Act, 1988.

Penguin Random House is committed to a sustainable future for
our business, our readers and our planet. This book is made from
Forest Stewardship Council® certified paper.

Set in Sabon by SX Composing DTP, Rayleigh, Essex

The Random House Group Limited Reg. No. 954009

www.**randomhousechildrens**.co.uk

Printed and bound in Great Britain by Clays Ltd, St Ives plc

Contents

Chapter One   7
Chapter Two   13
Chapter Three   25
Chapter Four   40
Chapter Five   47
Chapter Six   58
Chapter Seven   66
Chapter Eight   71
Chapter Nine   78
Chapter Ten   86
Chapter Eleven   93
Chapter Twelve   105
Chapter Thirteen   114
Chapter Fourteen   126
Chapter Fifteen   135
Chapter Sixteen   147
Cricket Commentary   154

Chapter One

Two weeks ago no one at Glory Gardens had even heard of Woolagong Cricket Club; now everyone was talking about it. Woolagong is somewhere in New South Wales, Australia. It can't be a very important place because it isn't in any of the atlases at school, but its cricket club is famous all over Australia: *This season Woolagong were NSW champions and voted best junior team of the year by the Australian sports writers* – that's what they tell us anyway, and even allowing for a bit of exaggeration it sounds as if they have some top players.

Of course, we'd have never known about Woolagong if it hadn't been for Ohbert. Paul "Ohbert" Bennett is Glory Gardens' number 11 bat, and he can't bowl or field either. People often ask why we bother with him in the team. There's no answer to that except Ohbert makes life interesting. His latest contribution to the club is The Glory Gardens Official Website. It contains some of the weirdest things about cricket you've ever seen, such as Ohbert's own strange theories on fielding positions and tactics and his reports of our latest games – all of which proves that Ohbert lives on another planet where they've never heard of cricket.

Although the site is called The Glory Gardens Official Website, none of us – apart from Frankie and Woofy – knew a thing about it until well after the damage had been done. That happened nearly six weeks ago when Ohbert sent out his challenge – an invitation to any club anywhere to play us for the title of "Undisputed Champions of the World". In Ohbert's dreamland Glory Gardens are the reigning World Champions and the top junior club in the Universe. Before we knew it Woolagong had accepted the challenge and, at this very moment, they are on their way to England.

Over the next fortnight Glory Gardens will play Woolagong four times: three one-day games, followed by a two-innings match over three days. They arrive tomorrow and the first game is on Sunday at Glory Gardens rec, the ground which gave the club its name when we started up two years ago.

Things have changed a lot since then; this is the team today:

Back row: Marty Lear, Jacky Gunn,
Bogdan Woof, Frankie Allen, Ohbert Bennett,
Matthew Rose, Kris Johansen
Front row: Cal Sebastien, Tylan Vellacott,
Mack McCurdy, Hooker Knight (captain),
Azzie Nazar, Erica Davies, Clive da Costa
Kneeling in front: Jo Allen

I'm Hooker Knight, captain of Glory Gardens C. C. Ohbert is in the back row, three from the right with the baseball cap and the Walkman headset. And Jo, our non-playing secretary, is kneeling in front. She's the one who plans and organises everything and she's been extra busy lately arranging all the details for the Woolagong tour.

Glory Gardens is more than a cricket team; it's a family. We've been very successful over the past two years and last season we won the under-13s League of Champions at the Edgbaston test match ground, so there is some excuse for Ohbert describing us as "the top team in the country". As Woolagong will find out, Glory Gardens has some stars of its own: Azzie and Clive, our best batters, and the opening fast bowling duo, Marty and Jacky. Another secret of our success is that we're packed with all-rounders; Cal opens the batting and bowls off-breaks; Erica is a great one-day bowler and solid middle-order bat; and I bowl left-arm seamers and usually bat at number five or six.

When Jo arrived at the rec that morning the rest of us were practising in the nets. Kiddo Johnstone, our trainer, was putting us through some fitness routines, so everyone was happy to stop for a moment to inspect Jo's final programme for the Woolagong games:

The Whitmart Tournament
GLORY GARDENS v WOOLAGONG
40-overs Competition

Match 1   2 pm Sunday, July 23
                  Glory Gardens Recreation Ground
Match 2   2 pm Wednesday, July 26
                  The Whitmart Priory Ground
Match 3   2 pm Saturday, July 29
                  Glory Gardens Recreation Ground

Three-day Match
GLORY GARDENS v WOOLAGONG

Friday, August 4 – Sunday, August 6
The Whitmart Priory Ground

"Why's it called the Whitmart Tournament?" asked Azzie. "Are they sponsoring it?"

"Yeah. Wally's getting very excited about it. He says England v Australia is what cricket's all about," said Frankie. Frankie, our regular wicket-keeper and team jester, is Jo's older brother. Walter Whitman, known to Frankie as "Wally", is the owner of Whitmart, the giant supermarket group. He's one of our keenest supporters and by far the richest. Whitmart have already paid for a new all-weather pitch at Glory Gardens rec and footed most of the bill for our brilliant new pavilion. Even Jo would admit that Frankie's unlikely friendship with the billionaire businessman has been worth his weight in gold to Glory Gardens.

"He's kitting us out with some new tracksuits and some Glory Gardens caps," continued Frankie. "He says we've got to wear the caps when we go out to field against Woolagong, because we'll be representing England and we've got to look good."

"It'll take more than a cap to make you look good," scoffed Cal.

"Very funny," said Frankie.

"If the one-dayers are called the Whitmart Tournament, what about the big game?" asked Tylan, our leg-spinner. "We can't keep calling it the 'three-day match'."

"It could be the Ohbert Challenge Trophy," suggested Erica.

"Catchy," said Frankie.

"What about Ohbert's Ashes?" said Mack.

"Yeah," said Tylan enthusiastically. "It's got to be the Ashes if we're playing Australia."

Frankie agreed and went into into one of his weird little war dances, chanting under his breath, "We're going to win the Ashes. We're going to win the Ashes."

"It'll make a change if you do," said Mack. "Even my dad can't remember when the poms last beat us." Mack is Australian. He and his family have been living over here for two years, since when he has been a regular in the Glory Gardens team. He's staying with me for the next two weeks because his parents are away on holiday; he didn't want to go with them and miss the Woolagong games.

"I bet England beat Australia next time," Matthew said defiantly.

"Only if we send over our beach volleyball team by mistake," scoffed Mack.

"Glory Gardens *are* going to win Ohbert's Ashes though," said Jo in a steely voice.

"Too right," said Jacky. "You'd better decide which side you're on, Mack. Is it England or Australia?"

"You don't need to worry about me, mate," said Mack. "I'm a Glory Gardens player okay; even being an Aussie comes second to that."

"If we call it Ohbert's Ashes, does that mean he has to play?" Marty asked.

Ohbert continued to nod his head to the tinny rhythm coming from his headset. As usual he was in a world of his own and didn't have a clue that we were all talking about him.

"Perhaps we could make Ohbert the trophy instead," said Tylan. "Then if Woolagong win, at least we'll have the consolation that they'll take him back to Australia."

"Good idea," said Jacky, with a laugh.

"That's just silly. Of course Ohbert has to play – he's part of the team, isn't he?" said Jo.

"Yeah, worse luck," Marty mumbled.

"Tylan's right, though," said Frankie. "We've got to have a proper trophy for Ohbert's Ashes too. I bet Wally comes up with a really flash one for the one-day games."

I looked over at Ohbert again and he gave me a blank grin as his head continued to bob from side to side to the Walkman's beat. I thought back to his astonishing last ball run out which had won us the League title a couple of weeks ago. Ohbert has the knack of being in the wrong place at the wrong time and doing the wrong thing, but for all his hopelessness, somehow it works out all right. I've seen him turn the course of a whole game in one mad moment. What, I wondered, would Woolagong make of our number 11 batsman who had brought them halfway round the world to play us?

Chapter Two

In the event, Ohbert wasn't selected for the first one-dayer. With the full squad of 14 all available, the selection committee of three – Jo, Erica, our vice captain, and me – opted for our best line-up for the opening game. That meant a six-strong bowling attack: Marty, Jacky, Tylan, Cal, Erica and me, and it left no room either for our other two seam bowlers, Kris or Woofy. Jo insisted, however, that all three of them should play at least one game in the Whitmart Tournament and that Ohbert should be an automatic selection in the next game. Neither Erica nor I was prepared to argue with her about that.

This was the team:

Matthew Rose   Mack McCurdy
Cal Sebastien   Frankie Allen (wkt)
Azzie Nazar   Tylan Vellacott
Clive da Costa   Jackie Gunn
Erica Davies   Marty Lear
Hooker Knight (capt)

We expected Woolagong to arrive on Friday morning but their plane was delayed for several hours and they had to stay overnight in a hotel near the airport. They finally turned up around Saturday lunch time with less than a day to spare before the first game. Jo went with Kiddo to arrange their accommodation, so she got to meet them first. Later, when we saw her at the rec, she had to face a barrage of questions. How many were there in the team? Who did she meet? What were they like?

"They looked pretty normal to me," said Jo. "Noisy and silly – like boys usually are."

"Do they all say things like 'G'day, sport' and 'That's bonzer, mate' – you know, like Mack does?" Woofy asked.

"Listen, mate, we speak bloomin' English in Aus," said Mack. "None of your posh pommy talk."

"Did you meet their captain?" I asked Jo.

"Yes. He's called Robbie Gonzales. He's got spiky bleached hair."

"Typical Aussie poseur," said Cal, giving Mack a playful shove.

"And their wicket-keeper? What's he like?" asked Frankie.

"His name's Slim Squirrell. They call him Slim because he's a bit overweight," said Jo, eying her brother.

Cal laughed. "The tale of two tubby keepers. And I bet he's nuts like Frankie, too. All wicket-keepers are."

"Squirrell's a good name for a nutter," said Tylan.

"Are Dai and Si still bragging about a 4–0 whitewash?" asked Woofy. Dai Holdright and Si Bannerjee were the two Woolagong players who had sent the first e-mail, taking up Ohbert's challenge.

"They sound confident enough," said Jo. "Dai says they haven't been beaten all season and they're not going to lose the winning habit now they're in England."

"I can't wait to see the look on their faces tomorrow after we've handed them out a giant-sized thrashing," said Frankie.

"They're arriving at the ground at ten o'clock tomorrow for a warm-up practice before the game," said Jo.

"And Wally's coming to welcome them," said Frankie. "He says he's not going to miss a ball bowled all fortnight. I think he's forgotten that he's supposed to be a multi-billionaire making loads of money."

"Did you know that Woolagong's sponsored by a supermarket group, too?" said Jo. "They put up most of the money for their trip."

"I wonder if Wally knows that?" said Cal.

"You bet he does." Frankie said with a grin. "Wally knows fat cats all over the world and I wouldn't be surprised to learn that he's been pulling the strings behind this tour all along. Only he'll never let on – he's too cagey for that."

"Is there going to be any food?" asked Woofy.

"Loads of it," said Frankie, grinning with pleasure at the thought.

"My aunt's helping out with lunch and tea," said Clive.

"Brilliant. Heaps of chocolate brownies," said Frankie, licking his lips and rubbing his stomach at the same time.

"If only it was an eating competition instead of cricket," said Cal. "Friar Tuck here would see them off single-handed."

"Then it would be called the Noshes instead of the Ashes," said Tylan.

"Why do they call it the Ashes anyway?" asked Woofy. "It's a weird name for a cricket competition."

"It goes back years and years, to the first test match. The poms lost to us," said Mack. "After the game someone burnt a set of bails and put the ashes in an urn. They said it was to mark the death of English cricket – and it's been dead ever since."

"And what about when Ian Botham beat you single-handed?" Matthew said defiantly.

"Okay, so we let you win every twenty years or so, just to keep it interesting. But Australia has won loads more times than England."

"Australia has won 117 test matches and England 93, with 86 drawn," said Jo.

"Like I said, loads more."

"Oh, but where are they now?" Ohbert asked, looking as if he'd suddenly woken up with a start.

"Where are what?"

"The Ashes?"

"They're still in the urn. They keep it at Lord's cricket ground," said Mack.

"Oh, I see," said Ohbert. I could tell he was thinking of something, but who knew what?

I didn't meet Woolagong's captain, Robbie Gonzales, until we went out to toss just before the game started. If there's one word that describes Robbie, it's "confident". He's got his mind made up about most things and he never holds back from giving you his opinion. Robbie was on the attack from the moment we shook hands in front of the pavilion and walked out to the middle to inspect the pitch. Something about his appearance reminded me of Shane Warne – maybe it was the bleached blond hair and the white lip protector. I soon learnt that it wasn't a coincidence.

"Who's the top world cricketer today?" he asked me suddenly.

I thought for a bit and said, "Sachin Tendulkar or Brian Lara?"

"No chance, mate," said Robbie. "Shane's in a class of one. He's got everything; skill, controlled aggression, brain. And there's never been a better tactician in the game. While Warnie's still playing, you poms don't have a chance of winning the Ashes. Did you see that ball he bowled at Lord's against Mike Gatting? I've got the video but I wish I'd been there to see it. And that beaut in the World Cup? Jeez, he turned the match against South Africa when we were on our way home." On and on he went.

Finally, to shut him up, I tossed the 50p and he called tails. It was heads.

"You can bat," I said.

"Okay, yeah, that's fine. I'd have batted anyway," said Robbie. "We like to get the runs up on the board. What d'you reckon would be a fair total on this mat?"

We were playing on the all-weather pitch, which is a good

batting surface but a bit on the slow side. In a 40-overs game I thought anything over 150 would be a tough ask. "200. Maybe 220," I said, without blinking.

"No probs," he said, shaking hands again. "May the best team win – as long as it's Australian."

On the way back to the pavilion we told the umpires that Glory Gardens were in the field. Jim Davy, who normally umpires for Croyland Crusaders, was standing in today for our regular official, old Sid Burns, who is on holiday. Jim's a strange bloke, a bit like a jolly old pirate. He slapped me on the back and said in his big, booming voice, "Good luck, matey. Don't forget you're playing for the honour of England and the Empire."

The Woolagong umpire was a thin man with a long, miserable face and a little black moustache. Jim introduced him to me as Mr Dryer. The first words I heard him speak were, "Will someone get that bloomin' dog off the pitch."

"Oh, don't worry about him," I said. "It's only Gatting, our trainer's dog. He's our team mascot."

"Gatting? Shane Warne would see him off then," commented Robbie, with a chuckle.

"You shouldn't allow dogs on the pitch. It's disgusting," umpire Dryer murmured crossly. I called Gatting and was a bit surprised that he waddled over obediently towards me. Together we made for the home changing room where I told Frankie to pad up. He nodded at me and went on with the story he was telling.

". . . and Si Bannerjee wanted to know why Ohbert wasn't playing. You won't believe this but they seriously think he's our star batter."

"Did you tell Si he was hopeless?" asked Jacky.

Frankie grinned mischievously. "No fear. I said we were resting him today, because of an old problem of his – a pain in the neck. But I told him Ohbert would be up for the next game and they'd be in for the shock of their lives."

"They've got two deadly fast bowlers," Tylan said, a little nervously.

"Yeah. Jack Grylls and Dean Caroota," said Marty.

"Dean's the one who hasn't got any clothes," said Cal.

"I didn't know they'd brought a streaker," said Frankie.

"He's lost his luggage, fathead. It didn't turn up at the airport – probably went on to New York or somewhere. So he's having to borrow all his clothes, and he's a lot taller than any of the others."

"So that's why he's walking funny," said Tylan.

"He was going to bowl in shorts, but I've lent him my spare cricket trousers," said Cal, who is the tallest player in our squad after Woofy.

"It'll be a bit of turn-up for your trousers to bowl with some zip," said Tylan, in a Tylanish sort of way.

Robbie gave Jo a list of the Woolagong players in batting order for the scorebook. There are 14 players in their squad – the same as ours – and I suspected Robbie had picked his strongest 11 for the first game, too. They were:

Dai Holdright	Cameron Armstrong
Ivan Susz	Mark Squirrell (wkt)
Robbie Gonzales (capt)	Si Bannerjee
David Larrington	Dean Caroota
Tom Stachiewitz	Jack Grylls
George Kynaston	

We took to the field for some warm-up exercises and catching practice. Marty marked his run-up carefully from the top end and bowled a couple of looseners at Tylan. Then the Woolagong openers walked out with the umpires and a trumpeter appeared from behind the pavilion and played "Waltzing Matilda". The Australians were delighted and cheered loudly.

"I bet that was Wally's idea," said Frankie, waving at Walter Whitman, in his trademark white suit and white sunhat, who had taken up his regular position under an M.C.C. umbrella by the trees. Wally raised his hat in a salute.

"Good luck, Glory Gardens," he shouted, grinning

with pleasure.

Frankie waved again. "I think he's more excited than we are," he said.

Kiddo was pacing nervously round the boundary, followed by Gatting, who was panting and struggling to keep up. Just below the pavilion, a strange little group of three, wearing funny masks, orange shorts and lime green tee-shirts were chanting, "Ohbert Bennett. Ohbert for England."

"Who are those weirdos?" asked Mack.

"I think it's Ohbert's fan club," said Azzie.

"Fan club? Why would anyone want to be a fan of Ohbert?" Jacky asked.

"Anyone who knows the answer to that hasn't been paying attention," Tylan said mysteriously.

We took up our fielding positions and waited for the Woolagong openers to walk out. There was that strange sense of tension in the air you always feel at the start of a big match. At last everyone was ready. "Play," said the long-faced Aussie umpire and the Whitmart Tournament had begun.

Marty raced in. His first ball was a fraction short and Dai Holdright, the opener, swivelled on one leg and pulled it square to the boundary. He grinned at Marty and walked out to the middle of the pitch to meet his opening partner. They tapped gloves in a little gesture of triumph – as if to say, First points to Woolagong. Marty stood and stared at them both. Finally he turned and walked back to his mark. The next ball was short and fast and whipped through under the batter's nose as he pulled away. "No-ball," snapped the Australian umpire, raising his arm to the scorers. Marty glared again – this time straight at the umpire.

I intercepted him at the end of his run-up. I had to say something to calm him down. "He likes playing off the back foot," I said. "Test him with a couple on a length. Get him driving."

"I'll try the yorker," said Marty, grimly.

It nearly found its way through, but an inside edge onto the pad gave them another run down the leg side. The rest of the over was straight and well-pitched-up, but seven runs were already on the board when Jacky opened up from the ditch end. We needed a wicket or a maiden; Jacky gave us the second. He nearly got the wicket too, but a fine snick just failed to carry to Azzie at first slip.

Marty started to work up some rhythm and pace but, when he dropped short, he was dispatched clinically to the square-leg boundary by Dai Holdright. Then the umpire no-balled him again, this time for overstepping. I was just thinking about giving him a cooling-down break when Mart produced the perfect out-swinger. It took the edge and Frankie pouched the catch.

Robbie Gonzales came in at three. It only took a couple of balls to see that he was the exact opposite of Dai. He was a left-hander and, at every possible opportunity, he rocked forward onto the front foot to drive. He seemed determined to dominate the bowling from the outset – even his defensive push had more than a touch of aggression about it. Twice Marty nipped the ball back at him and appealed for lbw, but their umpire just shook his head. To be fair Robbie was well forward on both occasions, but that didn't impress Marty.

Soon the Woolagong skipper was seeing the ball well and scoring freely against both Jacky and Mart, using their pace to drive cleanly on the off-side. Time for Tylan, I decided.

Ty spins the ball a lot, but he's not always in control of his length or direction. Gonzales was at the non-striker's end when he sent down his first delivery. It was short, but it turned sharply and the opener shaped for the square cut and got the thinnest tickle straight into Frankie's gloves. For a moment I thought the umpire was going to ignore Frankie's monster appeal, but fortunately the batsman nodded at the keeper and walked, and as he did Mr Dryer seemed to change his mind and slowly raised his finger.

"Not in the Shane Warne class," remarked Robbie to Tylan. "But it turned a bit. You wait till you see Si bowling on this."

We'd already heard about Si Bannerjee's leg breaks. He's Woolagong's top wicket taker and his name is down to join the famous Australian Cricket Academy next year. One day he'll be playing for Australia, following in the steps of Shane Warne, or so Robbie told us.

Tylan turned another and it fizzed past the incoming batsman's groping bat. His third ball was edged through the slips for a single. Robbie countered by sweeping a good length delivery fine for four. It was a class shot.

I kept Marty on for a fifth over, thinking that if we could nip out another, we'd be well on top. Twice he went past the edge to cries of frustration from Azzie and Frankie. But he kept his quickest delivery for the last ball of his spell; it beat the batter for pace, came back off the pitch and clipped the off bail. They were 40 for three.

"I need another fielder on the leg side," Tylan said to me, after Robbie had picked him off again, sweeping with the spin.

"I'll bring Azzie over to short fine-leg," I said. "If he keeps sweeping, I'll push him out for the top edge."

At the top end it was time to replace Marty. Both Cal and Erica are more effective bowling into the breeze, so I took on the job of trying to contain the Woolagong skipper. It wasn't easy. He was onto anything overpitched like a terrier, and if you dropped short, he was a fierce puller and hooker too. My first over went for four runs; I was relieved that it hadn't been more. At the end of it Frankie came up for a word in my ear.

"He's taken his guard well out of his crease," he said. "Give me a sign for a slower one and I'll come up to the stumps while you're bowling and . . . kerpow! Yet another brilliant stumping by Frankie Allen."

"I'll give my left ear a tug at the end of my run before I bowl the slow one. Watch out for it," I said.

"Okay. Try and keep it outside the off-stump and I'll be ready." Frankie lumbered back to his position behind the stumps, grinning contentedly.

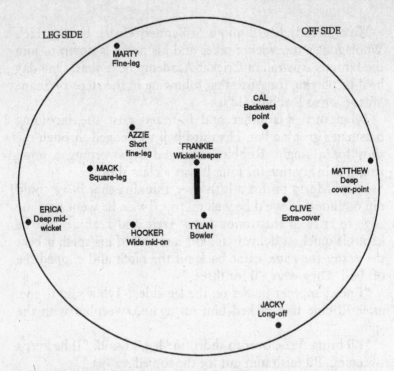

LEG SIDE   OFF SIDE

MARTY
Fine-leg

CAL
Backward
point

AZZIE
Short
fine-leg

FRANKIE
Wicket-keeper

MACK
Square-leg

MATTHEW
Deep
cover-point

ERICA
Deep mid-
wicket

CLIVE
Extra-cover

HOOKER
Wide mid-on

TYLAN
Bowler

JACKY
Long-off

Tylan's field, bowling to the left-hander.

I had to move the field about several times more for Tylan – my plan was to attack the right-hander and defend against the left-handed Gonzales. It was probably time for another bowling change, too – perhaps Erica could damp down the scoring rate. With my mind on all these things I completely forgot about my pact with Frankie. Before I ran in for the second ball of my next over I must have given my left ear an absentminded scratch. Frankie certainly thought so. As I came into the delivery stride and put everything into the quickest ball I'd bowled so far, I was appalled to see him wobbling up to the stumps at full tilt. The ball swung late and went past the inside edge of Robbie Gonzales's bat. Frankie yelped as the ball caught him on the top of the shoulder, flicked the side of his head and went for four byes. "What the—" he stammered. "Call that a slower ball?"

"Sorry, Frankie," I said, realising what had happened. "I wasn't pulling my ear though – I was scratching it."

"You nearly took mine off," said Frankie massaging his shoulder and head furiously.

The scoreboard was still racing, and by the time Robbie had driven me for another boundary through cover point, they were going along at more than four-and-a-half an over. 70 was on the board with 38 already against the skipper's name.

We weren't bowling badly – Tylan was going past the bat at least once an over – but we needed a break. Robbie edged Ty for two and swept him for two more. Tylan gave the next ball a lot of air and Robbie got to the pitch and drove to deepish extra cover where I'd just positioned Mack. The ball travelled fast and Mack swooped as they set off for the single.

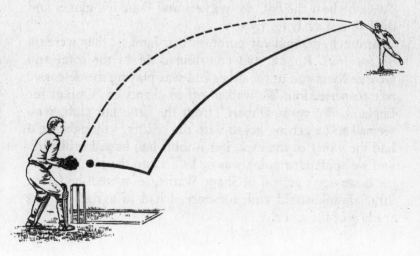

The lower the trajectory the quicker the ball reaches the keeper. Mack throws low and hard and the ball hammers first bounce into Frankie's gloves over the stumps. A higher, direct throw would have taken a precious fraction of a second longer.

He fired in a low throw which drilled into the pitch and bounced up perfectly just above the stumps for Frankie to gather and flick off the bails. "That's out!" screamed Frankie, pointing at the square-leg umpire who slowly, almost reluctantly, raised his finger. He needn't have bothered because the batsman had continued his run towards the pavilion.

Mr Dryer wasn't a bit pleased with Frankie's outburst. "I guess they don't teach you how to behave on a cricket field in England. Just keep your appeals to 'Howzat' in future," he said sternly.

After the run out the scoring rate slowed a bit, with the new batsman, George Kynaston, taking most of the strike. Tylan was bowling better and better. It was turning into a dream spell, except for the fact that he was having no luck at all. Twice he beat the bat, the wickets and Frankie's gloves and the ball ran away for byes.

At lunch, the midway point of their innings, they were on 88 for four. Robbie had contributed 46 to the total and George Kynaston at the other end was playing the defensive role to perfection. We walked off to chants of "Ohbert for England. We want Ohbert" from the little fan club, who seemed to be getting bored with the cricket. I thought we'd had the worst of the luck, but Robbie had batted brilliantly and we applauded politely as he led us into the pavilion.

"If we don't get rid of Shane Warne, soon we'll be facing 200," Frankie said and, for once, I had to agree with his reading of the game.

Chapter Three

"That umpire's not doing us any favours, is he?" Azzie said, with a nod in the direction of Mr Dryer, the Woolagong official, who was busy giving a lecture to Kiddo and Jim Davy – you could tell it was boring from the look on old Jim's big red face.

"Imagine having him umpiring for four whole matches," said Jacky. "I bet he never ever gives us an lbw decision," said Jacky.

"He was never going to give that catch off my first ball," said Tylan. "I couldn't believe it. Did you see the look on his face when their opener walked?"

"It's a miserable face, all right," said Marty.

Frankie laughed. "You should know, Dreary. You're the world expert on miserable." Dreary Leary is one of Frankie's nicknames for Marty.

"I'm not miserable," insisted Marty.

"That's like saying Tylan's socks aren't smelly," said Frankie.

"Who's on after lunch, Hooker?" Cal asked.

"Probably Erica. Tylan's got one more over and then it's your turn at the ditch end."

Frankie grabbed the last chocolate brownie, his eleventh, and mumbled something about the saddest thing in the world being an empty plate, before going off to put on his pads and gloves again.

"Are you ready, maties!" boomed Jim Davy, coming up behind Matthew and Jacky and slapping them both hard on the back. They nearly jumped out of their skins and he roared with delight. Jim's got a voice that sounds as if it's plugged into a massive loudspeaker. He's one of those people who think the louder they shout the better everyone will understand them.

We filed out onto the pitch again. I had tried not to eat too much of Clive's aunt's brilliant lunch, but one or two of the others – particularly Frankie – looked ready for an afternoon's snooze. I set a defensive field for Robbie Gonzales. If he was going to get his 50, he'd have to work hard for it.

Erica bowled tightly from the start and Tylan's bad luck continued to the very end of his spell. The Woolagong skipper got a leading edge, trying to force him on the leg side, and the ball spooned in the air and fell just short of a desperate lunge by Clive racing in from mid-on. Ty's final figures of one for 31 from eight overs didn't do him any justice at all.

It was Cal who replaced Tylan at the bottom end. Robbie was on strike, still needing one run for his half-century. He went down the wicket to the first ball of the over and aimed a shot over extra cover. The ball turned past the edge of his bat and Frankie fumbled an easy stumping chance. Cal put his head in his hands and groaned.

"Too many brownies!" shouted Tylan from square-leg.

Frankie threw the ball crossly to Cal and mumbled, "Sorry." He knew it was a big miss and two balls later Robbie posted his 50 with a confident reverse sweep. A couple of singles followed to bring up Woolagong's 100.

Robbie now went firmly on the attack. I considered bringing Marty back to replace Erica but, after being hit for a boundary, she kept her cool and continued to put the ball on a length and, above all, to keep it straight. Robbie kept driving but the fielding was tight and there weren't many gaps. Finally, out of frustration, he came down the pitch to Erica, lashing the ball on the off-side. I was at wide mid-off and it screamed over my head. I leapt in the air and was amazed to feel it thud into the palms of my hands. I fell backwards and did a reverse somersault but I hung on. It was one of those catches you take once in ten or twenty attempts. I leapt to my feet and in delight hurled the ball high in the air as the whole team rushed round me.

"Outrageous," shouted Tylan.

"What a catch!" said Erica. "It was going so fast. How ever did you see it?"

"I didn't. I just stuck out my hands."

"Thanks, Hooker," said Frankie, slapping me on the back. I knew what he meant. He was particularly pleased to see the back of Robbie Gonzales. When you miss a chance off a top batter, every extra run that he scores makes you feel sicker and sicker.

Suddenly the fielding was twice as positive; the bowling more aggressive. The sixth wicket fell in Cal's third over. The new Woolagong batsman went back to a straight one and missed. The ball thudded into his pad. "Halfway up the middle stump, matey," roared Jim Davy, raising his finger in response to the loud lbw appeal.

With ten overs of the forty remaining I turned to our twin pace attack again – with Marty bowling at the top end as before. Facing him was Slim Squirrell, the Woolagong keeper, who was showing all the signs of being a big hitter in the Frankie mould – except he had a bit more technique than our wicket-keeper. Marty raced in and put everything into his first ball. He stumbled in the delivery stride and fell heavily but the ball thudded into the batsman's pads. "Howzat," screamed Frankie and Cal at mid-off.

"Not out," was the Woolagong umpire's grim reply. Marty picked himself up and rubbed his ankle. I could see he was limping badly and I went over to him.

"I've twisted it," said Marty.

"Go off for a bit," I suggested. "I'll finish your over."

"No, I'll try and bowl off my short run." Marty hobbled

back to reposition his marker. His next ball was much slower, a leg break which went between bat and pad and definitely snicked something on the way through to Frankie. "Howzaaaat." Marty turned and appealed with both hands raised to the sky.

"Not out."

Marty looked stunned. He stormed back to his mark, still limping. This time, off the short run, he sent down a thunderbolt which knocked back all three stumps – the middle one flew out of the ground. He turned to the umpire and said sarcastically, "Nearly had him that time, didn't I?"

The score was 121 for seven. We had fought back well since lunch, but Marty's game was over, at least as far as bowling was concerned. His ankle was really troubling him and at the end of the over he went off. Ohbert came on as substitute fielder. He sidled on to the pitch to a massive cry of "Here comes Oh-bert!" from the fan club trio. Ohbert didn't seem to hear; he grinned foolishly and eventually found his way to third-man with a bit of help from Azzie. The three masked supporters moved round the boundary until they were standing right behind him and the chanting continued, getting louder and louder by the minute.

"Thought you said he was injured?" said George.

"You can't keep a real pro out of the game," said Frankie. "Wait till you see his fielding. It's electric."

With just six overs of the innings remaining, George and Si Bannerjee, the new player at the crease, started to go for their shots. I knew our best chance of keeping the scoring down was to snap up the last wickets cheaply. Jacky set the standard with a good tight over and then I came back to replace Marty. A big shout for lbw failed to get a flicker of response from the Australian umpire. The ball was straight and would have hit middle and leg halfway up – but by now I wasn't even expecting to get an lbw decision. The big question was, would he still give the batsman the benefit of the doubt when Woolagong were bowling?

I made the mistake of pitching just a fraction short to Si Bannerjee. Being small he loves to pull and hook and he stepped inside and dispatched the ball to the square-leg boundary. A couple of balls later I gave him a much quicker one on the same length and, attempting the shot again, he trod on his stumps. It was my first wicket of the match and a touch lucky. My second came next over when George Kynaston, who had been holding the innings together for a long time, at last holed out to Clive at mid-wicket. The last three wickets had put on an exasperating 40 runs at five an over, and numbers 10 and 11 continued to push up the total, scoring mostly off the edge of the bat.

One edge went straight to Ohbert at third-man. It wasn't travelling very fast but he let it roll through his legs. He turned, picked up on the second attempt and threw the ball straight back over his head for four. The fan club roared with delight and one of them threw the ball over his head back to Ohbert which gave the spectators something else to laugh about – although I wasn't amused at giving away four runs.

Three balls later Jacky's neat caught-and-bowled wrapped up the innings. They were all out for 163.

Back in the dressing room we found Marty lying on a bench, a bag of ice wrapped round his ankle. He told me he'd bat with a runner if we needed him, but the injury looked bad. Would he be fit in three days' time for the next game, I wondered? Marty had taken three for 24 from six overs and had looked in a league of his own. If we were going to challenge Woolagong, we'd need him bowling at his best.

The big topic in the dressing room, though, wasn't Marty's ankle but Mr Dryer's finger. "He's biased," said Jacky. "Anyone can see that. There were at least six dodgy decisions in their favour. And every one came from his end."

"I've just remembered who he reminds me of," said Frankie. "It's the moustache."

"You mean Charlie Chaplin?" said Tylan.

"No. Adolf Hitler. He's even got the same haircut."

"You're right," said Jacky.

"I don't suppose Hitler was a very fair umpire, either," said Tylan.

"They don't play cricket in Germany, stupid," Marty said scornfully.

"Perhaps he escaped to Australia after the war, and changed his name to Mr Dryer."

"Or Herr Dryer," Frankie said, laughing at his own unintentional joke.

Through the dressing room window I watched Woolagong's opening pair of quicks loosening up in the outfield. Jack Grylls was built like a rugby player, with enormous shoulders. Dean Caroota was taller and wirier, with long black hair that he kept flicking out of his eyes. Both of them looked fast and aggressive. You could feel the tension building as Cal and Matthew prepared to go out to face the Woolagong attack. They've both had a poor run of form lately and Frankie decided they needed a pep talk before they opened the innings. "This is our big chance, lads," he said. "Knock them over now and they'll never get up again for the rest of the series. Remember what Kiddo says, we've got to all play for each other. Think of the team."

"Just like you did at lunch with those brownies?" said Cal.

"I only had a couple of them. I'm on a diet."

"If you're on a diet, I'll eat my head," scoffed Cal.

The way Matt and Cal played and missed in the first two overs didn't inspire confidence. Jack Grylls was very quick. All his pace came from his shoulders and he bowled square on, swinging the ball away from the right-handers. Dean Caroota was even quicker. He had a very fast run-up and a slinging action. He hit the wicket hard and got good bounce – judging by the way Matthew and Cal were playing him, he was also cutting the ball back sharply.

With some sound defensive play and a big slice of luck,

Matt and Cal stuck together through the first eight overs. Cal was badly dropped in the slips and Matthew got the benefit of the doubt in a close run-out decision. They didn't trouble the scorers a great deal, however. We had crawled to just 15 when Gonzales introduced his spinner for the first time.

Si Bannerjee's first ball in England spelt big trouble. He ran in off just four paces and bowled a flighted delivery which brought Matthew prodding forward. It turned sharply, beat the outside edge and knocked back the off-stump. The Woolagong team went wild and Robbie Gonzales danced deliriously round his little leg-spinner. It didn't take too much imagination to guess what he was saying – "Almost as good as the one Warnie bowled at Mike Gatting!" Matthew walked off glumly with his head bowed. I knew exactly how he felt – all that hard work and no reward.

Azzie played out the rest of the over with great care. He's the best player of spin in the team and he says he can pick the googly and the top-spinner from the bowler's hand. If he couldn't tame Si Bannerjee we were in serious trouble.

Cal hit the first boundary of the innings, taking advantage of a rare long-hop from Cameron Armstrong, the new bowler at the ditch end. He came in off a short run but was deceptively quick. The scoring rate improved marginally, but, at the end of the tenth over, we still had only 29 on the board.

It wasn't the best moment for the TV van to arrive. A big green and yellow trailer pulled into the Priory car park and a man in a denim jacket with a large pair of headphones hanging round his neck jumped out. "Is this where the England lads are playing Australia?" he shouted. Frankie and Tylan shot off to investigate, followed by Kiddo and Gatting. Azzie, meanwhile, produced the stroke of the day, stepping back and carving the leg-spinner square to the point boundary. Everything about his batting is simple – he defends with a straight bat and punishes the bad balls.

The best players of spin bowling never push hard at the ball. Notice how Azzie relaxes the bottom hand's grip on the bat at the moment he plays the ball so that if he gets an edge it will not carry to the close fielders. It's called "playing with soft hands".

Since Matt's dismissal Az had faced every ball from Si Bannerjee, which was just as well because the leg-spinner was turning it a lot. But then he went and spoilt everything with a loose flick off his toes from a quickish half-volley from Armstrong. It flew straight to square-leg who took a sharp catch. Clive faced just two balls before he was needlessly run out. There was a horrible misunderstanding over a short single, which left Clive stranded in the middle. Although Clive blamed Cal, there didn't seem to be much doubt that it was his call. And it was hardly the first time that Clive had been involved in a silly run out.

No one took much notice of Clive's complaints because Frankie and Tylan returned. "It's our big chance to become stars," said Frankie. "Glory Gardens is going to be on the local news tonight."

"What for?" I asked.

"Someone's told them about Ohbert's Ashes," said Tylan. "They want to interview us."

"I bet it was Wally," said Frankie.

Erica fell to one of the worst umpiring decisions I've ever seen. Cameron Armstrong bowled an attempted slower ball but it must have slipped out of his fingers. It lobbed at shoulder height to Erica. Instinctively she went to swing it away on the leg side, missed, and the ball hit her on the top of the arm. Only the keeper appealed but Herr Dryer's finger was up in a flash. Erica looked stunned. Firstly, it was a no-ball because it was over waist height, and secondly, it would have passed well over the stumps. I saw Jim Davy take a couple of paces forward at square-leg, but then he must have decided against intervening and left Erica to her fate. We had slumped to 39 for four.

I went out to bat, calculating the run target in my head to help me forget about the TV cameras and the rotten umpiring. The asking rate was now more that five an over, but the important thing was to build a partnership and not lose another wicket.

"What's going on with those cameras? Are they making a film?" asked Cal when I arrived in the middle.

"It's the TV news – don't think about it again until you're celebrating your 50."

"Fat chance," said Cal. "This little spinner's tying me up in knots. He's turning it both ways. I just play everything as if it's a leg break. When it's not I miss by a mile."

"He's only got eight overs. Just hammer the bad balls," I said without much confidence.

"And watch out for the sledging," said Cal as a parting shot.

I leg-glanced my first ball for a single and was soon facing a new over from Si Bannerjee. There wasn't a single ball I dared leave, and I only survived the top-spinner with the help of a lucky inside edge which just missed the stumps and sped away for two.

Slim Squirrell, behind the stumps, kept up a running commentary on my batting and how useless it was. "Unlucky, Si. Far too good for him" or "Bowling, Si. Keep it there, mate. He's got no idea." I pretended not to notice. Finally I remembered to use my feet to the little spinner – dancing down the track to drive the last ball of the over to long-on for a single. "Keep it there, Si," I said to the bowler, when I got down to the other end.

Back came Caroota from the top. Robbie Gonzales had decided that if he nipped out a couple more at this stage the game was as good as won. The big bowler was fast. I didn't even see the first ball till it had whizzed past the outside edge of my bat into the keeper's gloves. Dean Caroota followed through, almost to the batter's crease, and glared at me.

"Another rabbit, Deano," said Slim the keeper. "I haven't come across so many of them since I read *Watership Down*." Deano growled and I walked past him and rather deliberately prodded the pitch. Somehow I knew the next one would be dug in short and I stepped back and hooked. I got enough bat on it to help it to the boundary. That felt much better and I played the rest of the over with growing confidence, in spite of the keeper telling me after every ball that it was time I was back in the hutch with the other bunnies.

From the non-striker's end I looked on helplessly as Si Bannerjee tormented Cal for five balls. It seemed almost disrespectful when he finally slogged the sixth back over his head for four. Cheers from the boundary greeted our 50.

The pressure was building, however. As we struggled to keep up with the asking rate I attempted to hook a ball from Caroota which he dug in very short, outside the off-stump.

It was a silly shot to play but the ball was way over my shoulder and I thought it was a free hit. All the time I was expecting the umpire to call no-ball – even as I gloved it. Instead he gave me out. Mark Squirrell bounced up after taking the diving catch and rushed over to congratulate the bowler.

The ball has bounced too high for me to hook and keep under control. The hook shot should be played with the body inside the ball, and you need to keep your eyes on it throughout the shot.

I stared at them. "What are you waiting for, sport? The third umpire?" said Caroota. I knew it wasn't out. So did they. If it's over your shoulder it's a no-ball in one-day rules. But there was nothing to be gained from arguing and I began the long walk back. I was met by Mack who was looking very pumped up.

"Tough decision, Hook. Don't worry, mate, I'll sort them."

Cal finally fell to a catch to the keeper too. Having survived seven overs and five balls of the leggie, he nicked the very last delivery of his spell, trying to force him outside the off-stump.

That was game over – or so we all thought back at the pavilion. At 64 for six, there was no coming back. But no one had told that to Mack and Frankie. Mack can bat a bit and Frankie has a wonderful eye and he's better than a mere slogger. They both set about the Woolagong bowling with relish, spurring each other on. Frankie got things going with a top edge for four over slip's head. Mack matched him, gloving an attempted pull over the keeper to the boundary. Then Frankie hooked for four and Mack produced an extravagant flat-bat drive which flashed through the covers and bounced up over the rope. The best shot of all was a cracking back-foot drive by Mack, timed to perfection.

The score was rattling along, faster than it had all day. Suddenly we were within sight of the hundred mark and players and spectators along the boundary were cheering every shot. It wasn't always pretty to watch – there were plenty of edges and wild air shots – but it was breathtakingly exciting. Cameron Armstrong stared open-mouthed when Frankie missed completely and the ball bounced down off his pads and rattled the base of the stumps without dislodging the bails. His next ball was straight and on a length and it flew off the middle of the bat over mid-wicket for four. Cameron then bowled Mack off a no-ball, only to watch in utter disbelief as his tormentor chinese-cut the next delivery for four more runs.

Signs of panic were creeping into the Woolagong fielding, too. Frankie was badly dropped and there were several misfields. But, sadly, the miracle wasn't to be. With the score on 108 Frankie played all round a straight one and his middle stump cartwheeled out of the ground. Then Robbie Gonzales brought back Jack Grylls who produced a lightning yorker to account for Mack, too. They'd put on 44 enormously entertaining runs together and, at least, saved us from an embarrassing hiding.

Marty hobbled to the crease and Mack stayed on as his runner. However, he didn't have to do any more running because a straight full toss trapped Mart on his back foot, plumb in front. Jacky survived a couple of overs with Tylan, but the end came when he too was adjudged lbw – another questionable decision by the Aussie umpire. We were all out for 120.

INNINGS OF WOOLAGONG.......... TOSS WON BY G.G. WEATHER FINE.

BATSMAN	RUNS SCORED	HOW OUT	BOWLER	SCORE
1 D. HOLDRIGHT	4·1·4	ct ALLEN	LEAR	9
2 I. SUSZ	1·1·1	ct ALLEN	VELLACOTT	4
3 R. GONZALES	2·2·2·2·2·2·1·1·1·2·4·3·1·2·2·2·1·1 1·4·1·2·2·1·1·2 (46) ·1·1·1·3·1·4·2·1	ct KNIGHT	DAVIES	60
4 D. LARRINGTON	1·2	bowled	LEAR	3
5 T. STACHIEWITZ	1·1·2·1·1	RUN	OUT	6
6 G. KYNASTON	1·1·1·2·1·2·1·1·2·1·1 2·2·4·4·2 1·4	ct DA COSTA	KNIGHT	33
7 C. ARMSTRONG	1·2	lbw	SEBASTIEN	3
8 M. SQIRRELL	2·2	bowled	LEAR	4
9 S. BANNERJEE	1·2·1·4·2	hit wkt	KNIGHT	10
10 D. CAROOTA		NOT	OUT	0
11 J. GRYLLS	2·4	c k b	GUNN	6

FALL OF WICKETS												BYES	1·4·1·1·2·1·1·1·1	14	TOTAL EXTRAS	25
SCORE	12	32	40	75	110	113	121	143	154	163		LBYES	1·1·1·1·1·1·1	8	TOTAL FOR	163
BAT NO	1	2	4	5	3	7	8	9	6	10		WIDES	1	1	ALL OUT	
												NO BALLS	1·1	2	WKTS	

SCORE AT A GLANCE

BOWLER	BOWLING ANALYSIS ⊙ NO BALL + WIDE													OVS	MDS	RUNS	WKT
	1	2	3	4	5	6	7	8	9	10	11	12	13				
1 M. LEAR							W							6	1	24	3
2 J. GUNN	M							4	4w					6·5	1	30	1
3 T. VELLACOTT														8	0	31	1
4 H. KNIGHT					M									8	1	29	2
5 E. DAVIES														5	0	11	1
6 C. SEBASTIEN				W										4	0	16	1
7																	
8																	
9																	

HOME TEAM GLORY GARDENS V WOOLAGONG		AWAY TEAM	AT GLORY GARDENS DATE JULY 23rd

INNINGS OF GLORY GARDENS — TOSS WON BY G.G. — WEATHER FINE

BATSMAN	RUNS SCORED	HOW OUT	BOWLER	SCORE
1 M. ROSE	1·1·1·1 >>	bowled	BANNERJEE	5
2 C. SEBASTIEN	2·1·2·1·4·2·1·1·4·1·2·1·2 >>	ct SQUIRRELL	BANNERJEE	24
3 A. NAZAR	1·2·1·3·4·2 >>	ct KYNASTON	ARMSTRONG	13
4 C. DACOSTA	>>	RUN	OUT	0
5 E. DAVIES	2 >>	lbw	ARMSTRONG	2
6 H. KNIGHT	1·2·1·4·2·2·1 >>	ct SQUIRRELL	CAROOTA	13
7 T. McCURDY	1·4·2·4·2·1·4 >>	bowled	GRYLLS	18
8 F. ALLEN	4·4·1·3·4·1·4 >>	bowled	KYNASTON	21
9 T. VELLACOTT	2·1·2·1·1	NOT	OUT	7
10 M. LEAR	>>	lbw	GRYLLS	0
11 J. GUNN	1·2 >>	lbw	KYNASTON	3

FALL OF WICKETS

	1	2	3	4	5	6	7	8	9	10
SCORE	15	36	37	39	62	64	108	108	108	120
BAT NO	1	3	4	5	6	2	8	7	10	11

BYES	1·1·1	3
L.BYES	1·2·1·1·1	6
WIDES	1·1·1	3
NO BALLS	1·1	2

TOTAL EXTRAS	14
TOTAL	120
FOR	ALL
WKTS	OUT

SCORE AT A GLANCE

BOWLING ANALYSIS ⊙ NO BALL + WIDE

BOWLER	1	2	3	4	5	6	7	8	9	10	11	12	13	OVS	MDS	RUNS	WKT
1 J. GRYLLS	:	⊙·	M	M	X	W·1	·							6	3	7	2
2 D. CAROOTA	:·	2·	·	2·	·	X	4·+	2·w	·4	X				8	0	24	1
3 S. BANNERJEE	W·	:·	4·	··	·2·	·	4·2·	2w	X					8	1	21	2
4 C. ARMSTRONG	:·	3·2	·2·w	·	4·4·	4·	X							6	0	35	2
5 G. KYNASTON	4·2	3·	·4·	w·2	1·w									5	0	24	2
6																	
7																	
8																	
9																	

Chapter Four

To be honest, the next day was no fun right from the start. I woke with yesterday's game on my mind and relived it ball by ball: Robbie's batting; the bad umpiring decisions; my ridiculous dismissal; Mack and Frankie's frantic partnership. And there were the other things too; especially Ohbert's strange, masked supporters and the TV crew filming the game. I tried to cheer myself up with a big bowl of Cocopops for breakfast. Then Mack appeared. He's staying in my sister's room, because she's gone off camping with some of her weird friends. Mack stared at me gloomily; he looked as if he'd just been told that he had been given double maths homework.

"Cheer up, Mack," I said. "Okay, we lost, but you batted brilliantly."

Mack shrugged. His face was a picture of gloom. Things didn't get any better after breakfast either, because he didn't want to be gloomy on his own. He followed me around like a shadow all day. When I spoke to him or asked him a question, I was lucky if I got a Yes or a No in reply – mostly it was just a grunt or total silence. I'd been really looking forward to having him to stay but soon I began to think that even Lizzie was better company. It was as bad as that.

"That's not like Mack," Cal said, when, at last, I managed to escape next door for a few minutes. "Perhaps he's homesick."

"Homesick? He only lives round the corner."

"Yes, but his parents are away. It's the first time he's been in England on his own. Maybe hearing all those Australian accents has brought it on."

"Mack's not the homesick type. He's too independent and . . . Australian. But he took some stick from the Woolagong lads while he was batting."

"No more than the rest of us. And Mack can handle sledging. He seemed fine after his innings."

"Not everyone would agree with you about the sledging. Matthew didn't like it."

"Maybe. I thought it was mostly jokey and good humoured – apart from Dean Caroota. He's got a mouth problem."

"He's a psycho – even some of the Aussie players think so."

"Frankie said he called Mack an 'effing pommy traitor' right in front of the umpire. If it had been old Sid Burns he'd have got a right earful for that, but Herr Dryer didn't say a thing."

"Jacky is convinced he's biased."

"I dunno. He gave some weird decisions – you got one of the worst – but that's a long way from calling him a cheat. I think he's just useless."

"I hope he's useless to them as well as us next time. Somehow, we've got to win on Wednesday and it doesn't help having bad umpiring decisions going against you."

"We'll win okay. Have you picked the team yet?"

"No. That's another thing. Jo wants to play Ohbert and maybe Kris. So, who are we going to drop?"

"Marty's still limping. It might be risky to play him."

"Fair enough – Kris comes in for Marty, then. And who do we leave out for Ohbert? We can't afford to lose a batter or another bowler. So Mack's my first choice."

"We'd miss his fielding badly. That run out yesterday was brilliant."

"I know. I don't want to drop him but—"

"Shhh. Here he comes," whispered Cal, nodding in the

direction of the garden gate where Mack was eying us both gloomily.

"Hi, Mack," Cal said breezily. "We're just going to watch the news on the telly. Coming?" Mack managed a nod and followed us silently into Cal's front room.

"You're right. He's not on full power, is he?" Cal whispered to me. "He seems to have turned into a zombie."

It was the last thing on the regional news, the bit where they usually say "And finally" and there's some stupid story about talking dogs or flying saucers.

First they showed a Frankie slog and Mack's cover drive, which looked really good – though Mack didn't show much interest in it. Then suddenly there was Ohbert peering out of the screen at us.

"Paul Bennett, I understand this latest England v Australia clash was your idea," said the reporter.

Ohbert grinned foolishly. "Oh but . . . er, yes, I think so." Behind him the Ohbert fan club trio were chanting, "Ohbert! Ohbert!" Close up the masks looked quite good; they'd caught the gormless Ohbert look perfectly.

The reporter was puzzled and distracted by the unwelcome attention Ohbert was attracting. "And who's going to win the, er . . . Junior Ashes series, Paul?" he asked uncertainly.

"Oh but we are. Glory Gardens, the Champions of the World," said Ohbert with a loony grin.

"Well, I have to say that you're not starting too well, are you?" The picture switched to a shot of Frankie's middle stump doing a spectacular cartwheel. "It looks as if Woolagong are going 1–0 up in this first game of the series. Can Glory Gardens and England bounce back on Wednesday? We'll be here to bring you the result."

On Tuesday the Woolagong team went off on a trip to London and we had a special coaching session with Kiddo in the afternoon.

"That batting performance wasn't good enough, kiddoes,"

he said sternly. "And if you don't get it together fast, you'll keep finishing second."

"But no one got out deliberately," I said, slightly stung by his criticism.

"I'm not saying they did. And the opposition bowled well, too," continued Kiddo. "But if we don't see a lot more commitment from the whole team we'll be out of this series by Wednesday evening. For a start, each and every one of you needs to play to a plan. And when you go out to bat you should be thinking about your plan all the time." Kiddo teaches us French at school, and sometimes he can't help slipping back into teacher mode.

"Did you see that four of mine on the telly?" interrupted Frankie.

"I did, kiddo. And I saw that dreadful head-in-the-air heave, too. I hope you've got it on video to remind yourself how not to play a lofted drive."

"We'd have won without Herr Dryer," Jacky said suddenly. "All his decisions went against us. Look at the way he gave Hooker out. That was the dodgiest dismissal I've ever seen."

"We all get bad umpiring decisions from time to time," said Kiddo. "And if you've got any sense you learn to live with them. You won't get anywhere blaming others for your defeat."

Without another word we got down to work. Kiddo put the top six batters through a net practice, with Jacky, Kris and Dave Wing, the Priory First XI's opening bowler, in one net, and Tylan, Cal and Kiddo himself bowling spin in the other. Each of us faced six balls of pace and then changed nets for six balls of spin. It took a lot of concentration to adjust to the change of pace and it also taught me to wait for the bad ball and then punish it hard when it came along.

The rest of the team concentrated on practising picking up on the run and throwing to Frankie over the stumps. Mack's mood improved a little; the fielding session seemed to take his mind off his problems for a while. He's such a brilliant fielder that I began to have second thoughts about the wisdom of dropping him for tomorrow's game. But it was too late now; the team had been picked and Jo was going to announce it after nets.

Mack is a great exponent of the sliding stop but he knows that if he can stay on his feet and pick up the ball on the run, he can save a vital split second. Notice how his foot is behind the ball as he picks up, offering a second line of defence. With the next stride he is straight into the throwing position, wrist cocked back to give him extra power in the throw.

Marty's ankle was still sore and he didn't take much part in the practice session apart from bowling a few leg breaks in the spinners' net. He had decided to rest up till the final one-day match on Saturday.

When Jo told Mack he was twelfth man he didn't complain. In fact, he didn't say anything but just nodded silently. I was beginning to think that any sound from him would be welcome.

This was the team for the game at the Whitmart Priory:

44

Matthew Rose	Frankie Allen
Cal Sebastien	Kris Johansen
Azzie Nazar	Tylan Vellacott
Clive da Costa	Jackie Gunn
Erica Davies	Ohbert Bennett
Hooker Knight	

"Good decision to pick Ohbert," said Tylan. "His fans were going to stage a protest at the ground if he wasn't in the team this time."

"They're not fans, they're more like the Barmy Army," said Marty.

"Ohbert's Barmy Army," Frankie said with a smile.

"They're almost as weird as Ohbert," said Azzie. "Did you see him on telly?"

"I thought it was a special effect," said Tylan.

"Yeah. Like one of those people whose mind gets taken over by aliens. *The Return of the Living Dead Ohbert*," said Frankie.

"What's that?" said Matthew, pointing towards the pavilion. The laughter stopped. A cloud of black smoke was belching out of the window next to the scoreboard and suddenly there was a strong smell of burning.

"It's a fire. The pavilion's on fire!" shouted Azzie.

I reached the window first. Through the thick smoke I could just make out a figure in the middle of the pavilion, jumping up and down and flapping its arms at a small fire on a table.

"It's Ohbert!" cried Erica.

Cal burst through the door with a bucket of water and threw it. Most of it sploshed over Ohbert. It took a second bucketful to put out the fire completely and Ohbert emerged sheepish and dripping wet.

"What on earth was going on in there, Paul? How did that fire start?" Kiddo demanded, putting on his most serious teacher voice.

"Oh . . . but I was making some Ashes," Ohbert whined. He looked like a coal miner at the end of a long shift.

"Ashes?"

"For the urn thing."

"I get it," said Frankie. "Were you burning bails, Ohbert?"

"There weren't any . . . but . . ."

"There's a half-burnt cricket stump on the table," said Cal.

"Oh but it caught fire very fast."

At last I understood. Ohbert had been making a trophy for Ohbert's Ashes. If we hadn't been there, the outcome would probably have been a pavilion-sized pile of ashes and a cooked Ohbert.

"You're not hurt, are you, Ohbert?" asked Jo, pointing at the large hole in the front of his revolting lime green sweater which had suffered badly from the flames. Ohbert shook his head and checked whether his Walkman was still working.

There was no real damage to the pavilion apart from the burnt table. Cal collected a few bits of soggy, charred wood and put them in a plastic bag. "Here are your Ashes, Ohbert," he said. "But finish making your trophy at home. Please."

Chapter Five

There's no better pitch in the county than the Whitmart Priory ground, where we were playing the second 40-overs game. So, when I won the toss, my mind was already made up – we would bat.

"It looks a belter," said Robbie.

"There won't be much seam movement or turn for any of the bowlers," I said.

"Not unless you're a true great, like Warnie," said Robbie. "He'd turn the ball square, even on this track."

"Lucky he's not playing then."

"It could be Si's wicket, too. He's not as good as Warnie, of course, but . . ." Robbie rubbed his hand across the surface of the pitch. "I wouldn't be surprised if he picked up a few today. He took two for 21 in the first game, and that's the worst I've seen him bowl all season. Is Ohbert Bennett playing?"

"Yes. He's really up for it today." Robbie was still worried about Ohbert's reputation and I couldn't see any reason to put his mind at rest. Maybe Ohbert's fan club had been talking to him about their hero.

"What number does he bat?"

"Er . . . I'm not quite sure yet. He usually likes to play well down the order."

"Like Lance Klusener?"

"Something like that. Mind you, Ohbert's not like anyone

47

else. He's a unique phenomenon."

"He's sure got a strange set of fans. Do they come to all your games?"

"Yes. He's got supporters from all over the country," I said, rather vaguely.

When I told Kiddo we were batting he didn't seem at all impressed. "Pity, I'd have put them in," he said. I was surprised at him, and annoyed, because he doesn't usually comment on my decisions, particularly in front of the other players.

Cal thought it was a bit off too. "I think Kiddo's more upset about the umpiring in the first game than he's letting on," he ventured.

"Something's making him grumpy, that's for sure," I agreed.

"Then we'd better get out and win this game – to cheer him up."

We had a team talk to remind ourselves of the game plan. I said we were looking to score 200, but 180 would be a good target. The defensive batters such as Matthew and, to a lesser extent, Erica, were to concentrate on looking for quick singles to get the flair players, particularly Azzie and Clive, on strike. We needed to take the game to Woolagong and get on top of the bowling early on.

Cal and Matthew gave us just the platform we needed against the opening attack. Matthew, in particular, had his fair share of luck against Jack Grylls, who went past the edge of his bat three times in succession in one over. But when the quicks came off after eight overs, we were 31 without loss; Cal had scored 18 and Matthew 10.

Just as it was looking as if we had snatched the initiative, Si Bannerjee took two wickets in an over. He bowled Matthew between bat and pad with his top-spinner which hurried off the pitch. Then, after his first ball to Azzie had been driven stylishly through the covers, he got the googly to straighten on him and Azzie played inside it. Herr Dryer signalled that it was out almost before Slim and Si had time to appeal for the lbw. Frankie was sure he'd heard a snick from the boundary.

"I bet you a fiver Azzie says that hit his bat first," he said. No one took the bet, which was just as well because he was right.

If Clive had any nerves at all, he didn't show it. He hammered his very first ball straight back over the bowler's head for four. He seemed to know that luck was with him today and he rode his fortune. If he hadn't been dropped at slip in George Kynaston's first over, the story of the Glory Gardens' innings might have been very different.

Clive times this shot to perfection. With virtually no effort he flicks a well-pitched-up ball in the air between square-leg and mid-wicket for four. Look at the position of his head – well over the ball at the point of contact, and his eyes follow it as it leaves the bat.

Above all, Clive took the attack to the the spinner, and his bold approach paid off. Si's next six balls went for 10 runs and the crowd was suddenly right behind us and cheering every shot. The score rattled up to 49 for two.

Ohbert's Barmy Army had now grown to six. Frankie said that if they kept doubling with every game they'd soon overtake the population of China. Tylan said he recognised a couple of them: two odd-ball kids from year seven who were in the school choir with him. This time the gang was camped on the opposite side of the ground to the pavilion, making most of the noise as usual. All but one of them were wearing Ohbert masks and they waved their baseball caps in the air as Cal scampered a single to bring up 50. But the chant was not for Cal or Glory Gardens, but "Ohbert! Ohbert!"

I couldn't make up my mind whether I found them irritating or amusing, but it wasn't possible to ignore them, unless, that is, you were Ohbert. He sat nodding to his Walkman, lost in Ohbertland and unaware that anything unusual was going on.

"It's hard to decide who's the most deranged, Ohbert or his fans," said Jacky.

"You have to be mad to understand, and if you're mad you don't understand," Tylan concluded.

Cal followed Clive's lead and went onto the attack. He knocked a boundary off the next over and then struck the spinner straight back over his head for another four. The pair of them were now well on top and Si, in particular, was proving expensive – he had gone for 30 from four overs. Finally Robbie was forced to take him off, but the return of Jack Grylls did nothing to stem the flow of runs. Clive treated him almost with scorn, pulling a fast ball only just short of a length to the mid-wicket boundary. The shot reminded me vividly of Brian Lara at his best.

"I don't think old Shane Warne's used to being under the cosh like this," said Frankie, as we applauded another boundary from Clive and watched Robbie fiddling with his field again. He posted two more players out on the boundary, but it made no difference. Another four took us through the hundred barrier, and now a state of near panic was spreading through the Woolagong fielders. Clive's batting seemed to rise to a higher level with every shot – I can't remember ever seeing him in such complete control.

"Cal is on 45 and Clive's got 44," shouted Jo from the scorers' box. 112 for two off 21 overs."

Cal plays the lofted drive with complete control. Notice how his head is well over the ball at the point of contact and he plays through the line rather than across it.

"No it's not, it's 107. You're wrong." It was Sepo, the Woolagong scorer, who was seated next to Jo. I'd hardly taken any notice of him up till now although Jo had said, after the first game, that he hadn't got much idea about scoring. It was also the first time I'd heard him speak; Sepo's voice was squeaky and slightly ridiculous.

Jo ignored him and put up the real total. But Sepo wouldn't let go. "Your score doesn't add up," he squeaked.

"Yes, it does," Jo said icily. "I'll show you your mistakes later. I'm too busy now."

A lofted drive for four by Cal took him to 49. It was probably the stroke of the day – no easy achievement with Clive playing a masterclass at the other end.

But did that shot lead to a touch of over-confidence? Cal tried to repeat the stroke to the next ball, which the bowler held back a bit. He hit it straight up in the air and the bowler turned, ran back and took an excellent catch over his shoulder. Cal slammed his bat furiously against his pad. He had got himself out one short of his first-ever 50 and he had every right to be angry with himself. Nevertheless, the 84 runs he'd put on with Clive had come at nearly seven an over. At 117 for three with 18 overs remaining, we were perfectly placed to go on to post a massive score.

Clive made no mistake about *his* 50 – hammering a short ball past cover point for four. Erica was then adjudged caught behind playing a ball down the leg side. She was convinced it came off her pad and stared coldly at Herr Dryer for a moment before departing. As she said later, "It'll make a nice change one day to end an innings by being really out."

I got a juicy full toss first ball and dispatched it to the square-leg boundary. Kiddo always says a bad ball is a bad ball, whether you've got none or 100 on the board. However, Clive didn't give me much of a chance to find out whether I was in form or not. He played a push shot into the covers and called for a quick single. If he'd set off immediately there would have been an easy run, but he changed his mind and sent me back. Too late. I wouldn't have had much of a chance of making my ground even if the throw hadn't hit the stumps directly. I was run out by yards.

Frankie stuck to his usual game plan. A wild whoosh at the first ball he received was like a manic windmill. It left him flat on his back as the ball missed everything and went through to the keeper. Frankie went down the pitch to the next and again his scything bat failed to make contact. He would have been easily run out if Slim Squirrell's underarm throw had hit the stumps. Instead, it missed by a coat of paint. The third ball found the middle of Frankie's bat and flew like an arrow straight towards us. It bounced just inside the boundary and scattered the spectators in front of the pavilion.

"Look out, Jo," shouted Cal. The ball flew like a Scud missile towards the opening in the scorers' box. It wasn't Jo it was targeted on, though, but Sepo. He stared out like a frozen rabbit, transfixed in horror. As the ball came for him, he made no effort to take evasive action. If Jo hadn't thrust out a hand at the last moment to parry it away, it would have got him straight between the eyes. Instead, the ball hammered harmlessly into the side of the box.

"Great save, Jo," shouted Cal and the Barmy Army roared their approval, too.

Sepo looked embarrassed. He didn't even say Thank you. Herr Dryer signalled the four and it was only when Jo acknowledged the signal that she looked at her right hand. The ball had caught her on the end of the index finger and it was already swelling up alarmingly.

"I'm not sure I can write with it like this," she said, wiggling it and wincing with pain.

"Mack, can you score for a bit?" I asked as Jo went off to the pavilion to find the first aid box.

Mack didn't reply but slowly got up from his seat, like an automaton, and took Jo's place alongside Sepo in the scorers' box.

Meanwhile, Frankie hoisted another mighty four over mid-on. The next ball from Cameron Armstrong was short and a little quicker. Frankie latched on to it greedily. He stepped back and pulled hard in the direction of the pavilion again.

There was a snick and then a softer, crunchy smack which instantly made me feel sick. Frankie dropped his bat and clutched his left eye. It took a couple of seconds before I realised he had top-edged the ball straight into his face. It looked serious and I rushed on to the pitch to help. Slim Squirrell shouted for ice and Cal, followed by Jo, emerged from the pavilion with a bag of it.

Frankie took his hand away from his face and grinned at me gruesomely. There was blood everywhere – running down his arm, all over his shirt, dripping on to his trousers. Most of it seemed to be coming from under his eye but there was a cut above too and the whole side of his face was swelling up.

"It would have gone for six if I hadn't got my head in the way," said Frankie, ruefully.

"Get some ice on it quick, kiddo," said Kiddo arriving with Cal and Jo. He wiped Frankie's face with a wet towel and offered him a glass of water.

"I know what you're going to tell me. I should have been wearing a helmet," said Frankie.

"Dead right," said Jo.

"At least it proves your head isn't as hard as we thought," said Slim Squirrell, drinking the water that Kiddo had brought out for Frankie.

The flow of blood was slowing and I could now see the cut better. It was about two centimetres long across the cheek bone. Frankie wanted to bat on but Kiddo wouldn't hear of it. "It'll need a couple of stitches," he said. "We're off to A and E."

Kris was padded up next and she came on to replace Frankie. As they crossed she took a good look at his eye. "You can blame the umpire and scorers for that," she said.

"Why?" asked Frankie.

"It was the seventh ball of the over. If Jo had been scoring it would never have happened."

Frankie and Kiddo left for the hospital and Jo went with them to have her finger checked out. A clatter of three more wickets followed their departure. Clive was caught-and-bowled for 67. There was nothing wrong with his shot, except it was centimetres off the ground and the bowler took a stunning reaction catch. Si Bannerjee came back on and soon bamboozled Tylan into making an error. Then, after a brief flurry of runs, he pinned Jacky in front of middle stump. So on came Ohbert to the biggest cheer of the day.

"Ohbert for England!" chanted the Barmy Army. And they kept up an amazing row throughout his innings, waving their baseball caps wildly and jumping up and down.

Robbie Gonzales went into a huddle with some of his players. There was no doubt he was puzzled about our star batsman coming in at 11, and he didn't quite know what to do. We were 165 for eight and very likely on the point of being all out for the same score. It was a disappointing total after Cal and Clive's brilliant stand had promised so much more. I reckoned we were 15 runs short of offering a demanding target.

Ohbert took no guard, and Kris told him that he had his bat round the wrong way. At last he faced up to Si Bannerjee. He played a couple of strange air shots to his first two balls from the spinner. The second went for a bye – it should have been two but Ohbert dropped his bat in the middle of the pitch and would have run himself out going back to pick it up if Kris hadn't yelled "Stay" at him, as if he was a disobedient puppy.

Woolagong were really confused now and, to my dismay, Robbie brought back Dean Caroota to bowl at Ohbert.

"He'll kill him. We've got to do something," said Cal.

"Such as?"

"You could declare."

But it was too late to save Ohbert from Caroota's first ball. It was fast and Ohbert met it with his low defensive shot, almost sniffing the ground. The ball hit him on the glove – he yelped and it shot through the vacant slips for four. Dean strode back to his mark and stormed in again. A rocket of a ball took out Ohbert's middle stump, but a no-ball had been called. Unbelievably, Ohbert wandered down the pitch to the next express delivery and swung wildly. There was a great roar as he connected with a thick edge and the ball flashed over the keeper's head for another boundary.

"I've changed my mind about saving his life," said Cal. "This is too good to miss."

Now Caroota was really fired up. He sprayed a wild ball down the leg side which went for four wides. Staring wildly at Ohbert, he spat out a mouthful of abuse. Ohbert just grinned and waved back. To add insult to injury he then proceeded to ignore the next three balls. Lifting his bat each time he watched calmly as they all missed the stumps by millimetres. The over ended with a single – another fine edge which deflected the ball off middle stump and beat the despairing dive of the keeper – to bring the score to 180. By now Dean Caroota was frothing at the mouth and we were laughing and cheering Ohbert's performance. His run tally had risen to nine.

Si Bannerjee would finish things off, though, or so we thought. Usually Ohbert misses every ball because he has no idea how to play straight. But now each delivery that Si bowled seemed to turn on to the middle of Ohbert's bat. It was as if he was psychic. If Si bowled the leg break he swung way outside the line and – *crack* – the ball lobbed in the air over point. If he bowled the googly Ohbert played inside the ball and it turned and flicked off the middle of the bat past square-leg. Six more valuable runs came from the over and the Barmy Army were so happy they seemed to be on the point of a pitch invasion.

The end was a bit of an anticlimax. Dean Caroota finally bowled a straight one. Ohbert waved it through like a toreador with a bull, and his middle stump cartwheeled. The innings closed on 187 and Ohbert, with a valiant 13 to his name, was carried off shoulder high by his exultant fans.

INNINGS OF GLORY GARDENS | TOSS WON BY G.G. WEATHER SUNNY.

BATSMAN	RUNS SCORED	HOW OUT	BOWLER	SCORE
1 M. ROSE	1.1.2.2.1.1.1.1	bowled	BANNERJEE	10
2 C. SEBASTIEN	1.2.1.4.2.1.3.1.1.2.1.1.4.1.2.2.1. 2.2.1.1.1.1.1.1.1.2.2(4⁵)4	c×b	ARMSTRONG	49
3 A. NAZAR	2	lbw	BANNERJEE	2
4 C. DACOSTA	4.1.4.2.4.2.4.3.3.4.2.2.4.4.1 (4⁴)4.4.3.2.2.4.1.3	c×b	ARMSTRONG	67
5 E. DAVIES	1.2	ct SQUIRRELL	ARMSTRONG	3
6 H. KNIGHT	4	RUN	OUT	4
7 F. ALLEN	4.4	RETIRED	HURT	8
8 K. JOHANSEN	1.1.1.1.1	NOT	OUT	5
9 T. VELLACOTT		bowled	BANNERJEE	0
10 J. GUNN	1.2.1.1	lbw	BANNERJEE	5
11 P. BENNETT	4.4.1.2.2.2	bowled	CAROOTA	13

FALL OF WICKETS											BYES	1.1.2.1.1.2.1	9	TOTAL EXTRAS	21
SCORE	31	33	117	127	135	156	157	165	187	10	L.BYES	1.1.1.1	5	TOTAL	187
	1	2	3	4	5	6	7	8	9		WIDES	1.4	5	FOR	
BAT NO	1	3	2	5	6	4	9	10	11		NO BALLS	1.1	2	WKTS	9

SCORE AT A GLANCE

BOWLER	BOWLING ANALYSIS ⊙ NO BALL + WIDE													OVS	MDS	RUNS	WKT
	1	2	3	4	5	6	7	8	9	10	11	12	13				
1 J. GRYLLS														7	0	29	0
2 D. CAROOTA														5.2	0	33	1
3 S. BANNERJEE														7	0	41	4
4 G. KYNASTON														6	0	25	0
5 C. ARMSTRONG														5	0	26	3
6 I. SUSZ														3	0	19	0
7																	
8																	
9																	

Chapter Six

The first thing was to find a substitute for Frankie, who hadn't returned and was, anyway, unlikely to take any further part in the game. Azzie volunteered to keep wicket and I asked Mack to come on as a sub fielder. He stared blankly at me as if he hadn't heard and for a moment I thought he was going to say No. But he shrugged his shoulders and went off to change.

In Jo's absence, Sepo the Scorer was still complaining bitterly about the extra five runs in her book. He'd got some of the Woolagong players to listen to him and they were adding up the batting and bowling figures and joking about how neat Jo's book was compared with Sepo's.

"You're wasting your time, Sepo mate. Jo doesn't make mistakes," said Jacky.

"That's right," agreed Tylan. "You, me and everyone else get things wrong from time to time, but not Jo."

But Sepo persisted and things started to get unpleasant.

"You'd think he'd be more grateful, after Jo saved his life," whispered Kris. Finally the Woolagong manager decided to inspect the two scorebooks. He eventually spotted that Sepo had missed a leg-bye and a four scored by Clive. We all remembered the shot – a drive between mid-on and the bowler. And that was the end of the story, for most of us. Jacky, however, wasn't in the mood to forgive and forget.

"Told you she'd be right," he said to Dai Holdright as we took to the field again. "Jo never misses anything."

"Yeah, sorry about Sepo," Dai said casually. "He tries hard but sometimes things happen a bit too fast for him and he loses the plot."

"Then why does he pretend he's the best scorer in the world?"

"Search me. He's never been able to add up," Dai said, strolling off to take strike against Jacky, who was opening the bowling at the top end.

"I'm certain he was trying it on, just like that umpire," Jacky confided to me. "What do you think?"

"I think we should bowl them out for 50, then there'll be no argument," I said. "Do you want a slip or mid-on?"

"Slip, of course. I'll probably need two when I get going."

Jacky bowled flat out for three overs and was unlucky not to pick up a couple of wickets. At the other end Kris strayed down the leg side a touch and Herr Dryer decided to get extra strict on the one-day wides.

The score was rattling along and, after six overs of seam, I went for spin at both ends. I had a feeling that Woolagong were more likely to get themselves out forcing the slow bowlers. This time my luck was in. Dai Holdright belted Cal to the mid-wicket boundary for four and then Cal struck back next ball, latching on to a very sharp return catch from the Woolagong opener.

Tylan went one better, claiming the big wicket of Robbie Gonzales, who was bowled off an inside edge for only two. That put us in control. Cal kept it tight at one end and Tylan, pitching well up and tempting them to drive, always looked dangerous. They struggled to keep up with the asking rate and the pressure mounted. As the shot selection became more erratic, the ball was flying about in the air. I kept telling myself that it was just a matter of time before one went to hand.

Finally Tylan turned his googly back into the number four bat's stumps. Next ball he lured the new batter down the wicket and Azzie finished off the job with a smart bit of stumping.

The scoreboard had been lagging behind without Jo to keep an eye on things and, as the fourth wicket fell, Jim Davy called loudly for a telegraph. There was a short break in play as we all waited for Sepo to put up the score – eventually 64 for four rolled up on the board. Old Jim glanced at his pocket book where he'd been keeping a note of the runs. "Get that scoreboard right, matey," he boomed at Sepo. "You've got four too many runs up there." After a short delay the total went back to 60.

"I told you he was cheating," muttered Jacky, loud enough for the Woolagong batters to hear.

I didn't say anything, but I was beginning to get a bit irritated with some of the things that were going on. My mood wasn't improved by Mack dropping a simple chance in the covers off Cal's bowling. By Mack's standards it was a sitter. I couldn't remember the last time he'd put down any chance, let alone an easy one like that. Mack was furious with himself and kept muttering and clenching and unclenching his fists. But in the very next over he fumbled a ball on the ground and then sent in a wild throw way over Azzie's head which cost us four overthrows. He let out a cry of anguish and buried his head in his hands.

"Come on, Mack. Which side are you playing for?" A familiar voice rang out from the boundary. Frankie was back – looking very sinister with a big black patch over his left eye.

Mack glared at him and when Cal went over to calm him down, he brushed him away angrily and stormed off.

George Kynaston knocked two fours in a row off Ty and I decided to turn to Erica for a bit more control. The scoring slowed but, as I started my spell from the other end, I realised that they now needed just five and a half runs an over for victory. Suddenly it was Woolagong who were taking control and we were losing the plot. Herr Dryer was still handing out ridiculous wides, virtually every over, at the top end. Another dropped catch – this time it was Jacky at square-leg – brought groans from the other fielders. Heads were going down and the fielding was getting more and more ragged. I had to do something, and fast.

George slogged me over mid-wicket for four and brought up the hundred. Frankie went to retrieve the ball and clapped his hands urgently from the boundary. "Get it together, Glory Gardens," he shouted unhelpfully. The OBA, as everyone now called Ohbert's Barmy Army, started a loud chant of "Give the ball to Ohbert".

I strengthened the off side with four in the ring and Kris on the cover boundary and dropped Clive out to deep mid-wicket. My plan was to bowl an off-stump line, moving the ball away, and tempting the batter to drive in the direction of mid-on, where there was a big gap to aim for.

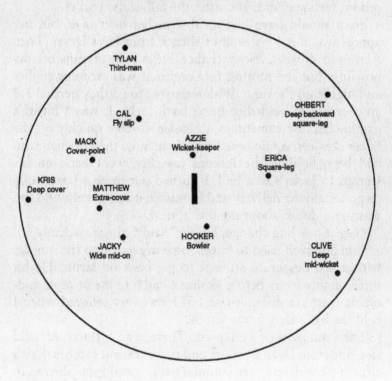

Once in a while you change round the field and get an immediate reward which makes you look like a genius. George rocked on to the front foot and drove at a wide half-volley. The ball looped off the outside edge of his bat, straight into the hands of Cal at fly-slip. He took the catch and grinned back at me.

"Some people are just born lucky," he said.

"All part of the plan," I said casually. "Though if I'd known he was going to hit it to you I'd have put a good fielder there."

There was a short break as the TV van arrived and the entire crew filed behind the bowler's arm with Jim Davy waving at them furiously and shouting colourful insults. I could see Frankie telling the reporter the story of the match so far, even though he'd missed most of the action.

"Let's show them we can finish it in style," I said to the others, feeling a bit better after the fall of the wicket.

Erica should have had an lbw in her next over, but her appeal was met by a wall of silence from Herr Dryer. Then Azzie put down a tricky chance behind the stumps off my bowling. But the scoring rate required was creeping higher and higher all the time. With ten overs to go they needed 7.3 an over and I decided to bring back Jacky. It was a bit of a gamble because sometimes it's easier to score quickly off the faster bowlers. Again I got lucky. Ivan Susz, their opener, who had been holding the innings together, went back on his stumps to Jacky's first ball. It turned out to be a beautifully disguised slower delivery and he missed it completely. Old Jim was in no doubt about the lbw appeal.

"Great bowling change, Hook," said Cal, sarcastically.

Slim Squirrell tried to inject some urgency into the innings with a last desperate attempt to get back on terms. He hit three mighty fours before skying a catch to me at deep mid-off. It wasn't a difficult one but I was very relieved when I held the ball safely in my hands.

The innings then collapsed. There was a flurry of wild slogging from Dean Caroota and two excellent catches. Kris's effort on the deep cover boundary was a real gem. She ran in 20 yards and still had to dive forward to get her hands under the ball. Dean Caroota was caught behind by Azzie, top-edging an ambitious pull shot. Then, with the TV camera lined up right behind him, Ohbert, as usual, stole the show. The champagne moment came from what turned out to be the last ball of the innings. Ohbert chased a ball back to the long-on boundary and ran straight past it. Then he turned and stepped on it, just before it crossed the line. As he launched himself into a sort of backward somersault he somehow managed to kick the ball with his other foot straight to Erica who was following up behind him. Her flat, accurate throw to the keeper was too good for the batsman who had set off for the third run.

Jacky's clever change of pace fools the batsman into playing far too early. The right arm comes through at the normal speed but he holds the ball back by releasing it from the side of his hand like a leg break.

The OBA picked up a squeaking and protesting Ohbert and gave him another bumpy shoulder ride back to the pavilion. Woolagong had crumbled to 140 all out. As we walked off I was pleased to see a lot of depressed-looking faces peering out from the pavilion. The applause for our win was no more than polite and Robbie Gonzales didn't even bother to come out and shake hands with me. I didn't mind that. It meant we'd go into the third game with the psychological edge. For the first time I felt Glory Gardens was calling the shots.

HOME TEAM	GLORY GARDENS V WOOLAGONG	AWAY TEAM	AT WHITMART PRIORY DATE JULY 26TH

INNINGS OF W.O.O.L.A.G.O.N.G. .... | TOSS WON BY GG ..... WEATHER SUNNY

BATSMAN	RUNS SCORED	HOW OUT	BOWLER	SCORE
1 D. HOLDRIGHT	2·1·2·1·4·2·1·3·4	Ct b	SEBASTIEN	20
2 I. SUSZ	1·2·2·1·1·1·2·1·2·1·1·2·1·4·2·1 2·2	lbw	GUNN	29
3 R. GONZALES	2	bowled	VELLACOTT	2
4 D. FITCH	1·3·2·4	bowled	VELLACOTT	10
5 T. STACHIEWITZ		st NAZAR	VELLACOTT	0
6 G. KYNASTON	2·1·4·4·1·2·2·4·1·1·2·4	ct SEBASTIEN	KNIGHT	28
7 L. H-KIRBY	4·1·1·1·2·2·1·1·1	RUN	OUT	14
8 M. SQUIRRELL	4·4·4	ct KNIGHT	DAVIES	12
9 S. BANNERJEE		ct JOHANSEN	GUNN	0
10 D. CAROOTA	3	ct NAZAR	GUNN	3
11 J. GRYLLS	2	NOT	OUT	2

FALL OF WICKETS											BYES	4·1·1·1·1	8	TOTAL EXTRAS	20
SCORE	35	38	60	60	100	115	128	133	138	140	LBYES	2·1·1	4	TOTAL	140
	1	2	3	4	5	6	7	8	9	10	WIDES	1·1·1·1·1·1·1	7	FOR	ALL
BAT NO	1	3	4	5	6	2	8	9	10	7	NO BALLS	1	1	WKTS	OUT

SCORE AT A GLANCE

BOWLER	BOWLING ANALYSIS ⊙ NO BALL + WIDE													OVS	MDS	RUNS	WKT
	1	2	3	4	5	6	7	8	9	10	11	12	13				
1 J. GUNN				X	W·4		W							5 2	0	20	3
2 K. JOHANSEN				X										3	0	17	0
3 C. SEBASTIEN			M		M				X					8	2	19	1
4 T. VELLACOTT	W	⊙			W·4				X					7	0	32	3
5 E. DAVIES						4W								7	0	31	1
6 H. KNIGHT		W	M		X									4	1	9	1
7																	
8																	
9																	

Chapter Seven

Frankie, with his black eye patch, peered round the dressing room door and grinned. "Well played, me hearties," he drawled in a piratical sort of voice. "Pity about the fielding, though."

"What about it?" asked Cal.

"It was rubbish."

Mack squared up to Frankie. "Keep your opinions to yourself," he said. "Or you'll have a patch over both eyes. Understood?"

"The last man who talked to Black Jake like that walked the plank," Frankie said, thinking that Mack was joking.

"Listen, mate. What right has a thicko like you got to tell me I'm not trying. I try harder for the team than anyone. And I don't make a habit of dropping catches like some I know." It was the longest speech Mack had made in days.

"Only joking," Frankie said, but he couldn't leave it at that. "I didn't say anything about not trying. It's just that you don't usually field like Ohbert."

"I'm warning you, Frankie. I'll give you—"

Cal pushed between them. "Cut it out, you two. What have you got to fight about? We just won, didn't we?"

"Behave, Francis," Jo said crossly. With a big white bandage on her right hand, she was doing her best to copy the scores neatly into her book. "Your writing's hopeless, Mack. I can't even read the names."

"It's upside down; that's how Aussies write," said Tylan. Mack scowled, but he'd lapsed back into silence again.

"At least yours adds up," Jo said, with a sigh. "Sepo's got their total as 144 instead of 140 and the bowling figures come to 148. I think he's added all the wides and no-balls in twice."

"It's funny how when Sepo makes a mistake it's always in favour of Woolagong," said Jacky.

"You mean he's cheating, like Herr Dryer?" said Tylan.

"Of course he is. They might as well have two extra players in their team," Jacky said sourly.

"You want to be careful accusing people of cheating when you've got no proof," said Cal.

"What more proof do you want? Ask Erica about that so-called catch by the keeper. It was nowhere near her bat – they all knew that, including the umpire."

"It was just a mistake, not cheating."

"What about my lbw, then?"

Cal laughed. "That was plumb. I'd have given you out from the pavilion."

"I'm with Jacky," said Clive. "There's definitely something funny going on."

"And the sledging's not fair, either," said Matthew.

"It's just the way Australians play cricket," said Azzie.

"I don't care if they turn up with fifteen players and a talking kangaroo, we're still going to beat them," said Frankie. "It's the first time Shane Warne and his gang have lost in a year. And, I tell you, they didn't like it."

"Right," said Cal. "The best way to answer sledgers is to give them a good hiding."

Kiddo appeared at the door of the pavilion. "That TV reporter says he wants to interview the two captains. What do you say, Harry?"

"Fine by me," I said, suddenly feeling very nervous but not wanting the others to notice.

"Tell 'em, Black Jake vows to scupper them on Saturday,"

said Frankie. "They'll wish they'd never put to sea."

"Oh but . . . they didn't, Frankie. They came on a plane," said Ohbert.

Kiddo led me to the side of the pavilion where Robbie Gonzales was already talking to the reporter.

"Hi, it's Harry, isn't it?" said the reporter. He was a short, red-faced man in a shiny blue suit.

I nodded.

"Great. I just want to ask you, and young Robbie here, a couple of questions about the game, nothing difficult, mind. He pointed a microphone at me. "Can you say something into this for me, Harry. Don't be nervous."

I coughed and said, "What shall I say?"

"That's great. It's just to get the sound right." The camera moved closer and the interview began. "I've got the winning and the losing captains of today's game with me here," the reporter said in a completely different sort of voice. "Harry, you must be very pleased to have fought back to level the series."

"Er, yes," I said.

"What did you think of the Glory Gardens batting today, Robbie?"

"They batted okay, but we let ourselves down. We'll have no trouble bouncing back at the weekend, you'll see." Robbie sounded very confident; he seemed to have recovered completely from the defeat.

"I understand there's a bit of aggro building up between the two teams. Is that right, Harry?" With a sneaky smile, the reporter pointed the microphone at me again.

"What?"

"Aggro? Bad feeling?"

"I know what aggro means," I said, a touch irritably. "And there isn't any."

"That's right," agreed Robbie. "There's been a bit of banter out there but that's all."

"You mean sledging?"

"Yeah. We like to make it tough for the oppo – to test whether they can handle the pressure. You should hear Warnie sometimes."

"Shane Warne?"

"Yeah, he's a top sledger."

There was no stopping Robbie after that; he was off on his favourite topic and the reporter couldn't get another word in. But why had he asked me that question, I wondered? Had someone been talking to him? Jacky, for instance? I could just imagine how Dean Caroota would react if someone told him that we thought they were a bunch of cheats. It wouldn't take much more of this to wreck the whole series.

"Well, er . . . thank you both for your views and may the best team win on Saturday," said the exhausted reporter, finally winding up the interview with a sickly smile straight at the camera.

"We will," said Robbie. I got the feeling he'd done telly interviews before and I felt more stupid than ever about my feeble answers as the camera moved in for a close up of us both.

When the selection committee met later I told Erica and Jo that the bad feeling between the two teams was getting beyond a joke, and they both agreed.

"The trouble is that we haven't really got to know them properly," said Erica. "The teams haven't been together at all apart from when we're playing."

"Francis thinks we should have a barbecue," said Jo.

"He would."

"It's not a bad thought – Australians like barbecues."

"And we could have a quiz night, too," suggested Jo.

"Good idea. Make it a cricket quiz. With Azzie in our team we'd be bound to win," I said.

Erica laughed. "That's typical. We're talking about being more friendly and sociable and all you can think about is beating them.

"But . . ." I began.

"Mack would be good too," said Jo. "He's brilliant on cricket history."

"I'm not sure he's in the mood," I said. "He told Cal he doesn't even want to play."

"I wish I knew what was bothering him," said Erica. "He's hardly spoken since the Australians arrived. You'd think he'd be pleased to get to know some guys from back home, but he doesn't go near them.

"Francis is out too," said Jo. "He can't keep wicket with one eye. And Marty's still having trouble with his ankle. There's not much chance he'll be properly fit."

So it came down to a straight choice between Mack and Ohbert. Jo said that if Ohbert wanted to play and Mack didn't, then that was fine. We made Mack twelfth man and selected a team with an enormously long batting tail:

Matthew Rose	Kris Johansen
Cal Sebastien	Tylan Vellacott
Azzie Nazar	Jacky Gunn
Clive da Costa	Bogdan Woof
Erica Davies	Ohbert Bennett
Hooker Knight	Twelfth man: Mack McCurdy

70

Chapter Eight

Saturday morning started dull and gloomy, and the weather forecast promised rain. It wasn't cricket weather and hardly anyone turned up to watch. Wally was there, of course, but even the OBA, back down to the original three, seemed quiet and subdued.

Woolagong won the toss and Robbie chose to bat, but just as we began to walk out to field the first downpour came, and it was a heavy one.

"Typical rotten English weather," moaned Dai Holdright as we all scampered back to the pavilion.

"Sledge us as much as you like, but I'd leave our weather out of it if I were you," said Frankie. "It can be a lot nastier than you can."

Frankie was playing because Azzie hadn't arrived for the start of the game. It wasn't like him to be late or not let us know if something had happened. Jo tried to call him at home, but there was no reply. Without Azzie to keep wicket, Frankie decided to take his chance and play after all.

"Don't worry, Hook," he said. "I can keep wicket with one eye."

"That's strange, 'cause you can't do it with two," said Cal.

Jo said the doctor had told him not to play and that he was being really silly.

"That's what I'm good at," Frankie said, winking with his good eye. "But even a one-eyed keeper is better than nothing."

There was no one else to stand in for Azzie, because Mack, who was supposed to be twelfth man, had done a disappearing trick. He'd come to the ground with me but now he was nowhere to be seen. So Frankie was back in the team.

It rained for nearly an hour and then stopped. The light was still pretty bad, however, when Jim Davy and Herr Dryer strolled out to the middle to inspect the pitch. Another half-hour was lost while sawdust was brought out for the bowlers' run-ups and we waited for the pitch to dry out a bit.

"It's 25 overs a side now, maties," Jim Davy announced loudly from the steps of the pavilion. "Maximum five overs for each bowler. And if we get any more rain we play the Duckworth-Lewis rules. I don't understand them, but Mr Dryer says he does. Is that agreed?"

"Duck with what?" asked Frankie.

"Don't be ignorant, Francis," hissed Jo. "The Duckworth-Lewis method. It's the way we work out rain-affected games."

"How?" asked Woofy.

"It's simple," said Jo. "You have a set of tables and a calculator and you readjust the target according to the resource percentage."

"Outrageous," said Tylan. "Is that instead of playing cricket?"

"Of course not, silly. If the number of overs are cut again you have to take into account overs and wickets remaining and the winner is decided by whether the revised target has been exceeded."

"Oh, dead simple, then," said Frankie. "Why didn't you say that in the first place?"

"Do you have the tables, Jo?" I asked.

"Of course. Leave it to me. You go and bowl them out."

At last the game got underway. Dai Holdright and Ivan Susz, the Woolagong openers, walked slowly out to the middle, staring up at the black clouds.

"It's the worst light I've ever played in," moaned Dai. "Do you often get weather like this?"

"I've warned you, you'll be struck by lightning if you keep complaining," said Frankie. "And watch out for the dead-man's skull beetles."

"What are they?"

"Huge, black, smelly things as big as your hand. Don't you have them in Australia?"

"N-n-no."

"They're horrible. They fly out of those trees over there in bad weather – thousands of them. And the vampire bats wake up too when it's dark like this."

"You're joking, aren't you, mate?" Dai said, looking apprehensively up at the poplars at the ditch end of the ground and then calling for his guard.

"There's one behind you right now," Frankie said, suddenly touching Dai on the neck. Dai nearly jumped out of his cricket pads.

It was lucky for Woolagong that Marty wasn't playing. His extra pace would have given them some big problems in this light. Marty had come along to support us and he told me his ankle was a lot better so he'd definitely be fit for the test match, but that was no help to us today.

The plan was for all the bowlers to stick to a line on or just outside off-stump – except for Tylan, who is a naturally attacking leggie and at his best when he pitches on leg and middle.

I opened the bowling with Jacky and Woofy. Woofy bowled well but, as usual, his long legs and arms seemed to run out of energy and he was gasping for breath after two overs. I replaced him at the Herr Dryer end with Kris. It turned out to be a brilliant bowling change because she immediately dismissed both the openers in her first over. Dai Holdright fell to a stunning catch by Cal at slip and three balls later Clive, at mid-wicket, took a sharp catch from the other opener as he drove in the air.

"Nightmare start, skipper," Frankie said mischievously to Robbie Gonzales, who was about to face Jacky for the first time.

"No worries, mate," retorted Robbie.

"I bet you don't get double figures," Frankie taunted.

"You're on then."

"And I bet you don't get as many as me."

"You're double on."

Jacky's first ball thundered into the Woolagong captain's pads and Frankie appealed loud and long. "A bit optimistic, matey," shouted old Jim.

"Optimistic? I'd have walked if it'd been me," said Frankie.

Frankie kept up the chat all the time that Robbie was at the wicket. It was like a battle of wills. Robbie got the upper hand when he belted Jacky through mid-off for four. Then Frankie bounced back with a barrage of insults every time the Woolagong skipper played and missed.

The verbal struggle came to a head in Kris's third over. The score stood at 23 for two and Robbie's personal tally was nine. A quickish ball, short of a length, cut into him as he played back. His bat was well away from his body and there was definitely a sound as the ball went through to Frankie. The whole team went up for a catch behind the wicket. Frankie's own appeal was deafening. But the grin of victory disappeared from his face when Herr Dryer remained unmoved.

Frankie threw the ball to the ground angrily. "That's not how we play cricket over here," he said to Robbie.

"What do you mean, mate. I didn't touch it, honest," Robbie said innocently.

"Oh, sorry. It must have been a mole playing conkers that I heard. We get a lot of them at this time of year. The bet's off, mate."

"Suit yourself. But I tell you, I didn't hit it."

I turned to the spin of Tylan, but Ty had one of his off days and he went for 16 in two overs. I switched again – this time to Cal's off-breaks. I was now bowling instead of Kris at the ditch end. Coming into the wind, I was getting the ball to swing a long way. At first I found it difficult to control and but soon I had the away-swinger going beautifully.

They pushed the score steadily up to 59, and then Cal got the breakthrough – George Kynaston looped an easy catch back to him off a leading edge.

The new batsman, Stacks Stachiewitz, slammed his first ball from Cal straight back over the bowler's head for four. With ten overs to go I knew that an over or two of big hitting could knock us well off course, but I kept bowling and fielding to my off-stump plan. I dropped a couple more fielders out on to the boundary and told Frankie to gee everyone up for the final effort. As the noisiest member of the squad, he has his uses sometimes. "Great throw, Clive. Keep them coming," he cried as a chase and throw from the boundary stopped Woolagong from taking a third run.

At last I got an in-swinger dead on target and bowled Stacks through the gate. Robbie, who had been off strike for some time, now started an all-out assault on Cal's off-spin. He went down the pitch to him and a big, lofted drive brought him another boundary. Then he played a fine sweep, and a reverse sweep, which went through Ohbert's legs for four. 11 came off the over; it was time for Erica.

Erica and I bowled wicket to wicket and, with the help of some lively fielding, the run feast became more of a snack. The final ball of my spell brought me a bonus wicket when the new batsman snicked an excellent out-swinger to Frankie.

Erica opened the next over with her slower ball, which is very slow indeed; Frankie knew it was coming and crept up to the stumps as she ran in, unnoticed by Robbie. The ball looped in the air and Robbie leapt forward greedily to smash it over long-on. But he played right over the top of it and turned quickly to ground his bat behind the crease – only to see, to his horror, the grinning face of Frankie and his bails flying in the air. The big appeal was answered with a nod and a raised finger by Jim Davy at square-leg.

"Oh, look what those moles have done to your stumps," Frankie said to Robbie, shaking his head sadly. For once the Woolagong captain was lost for words.

Slim Squirrell went for a huge, ugly slog and was comprehensively bowled. Three wickets had fallen on 91 and, with just two overs remaining, I brought back Woofy. His first ball, a long hop, was dispatched for four. Then he produced the yorker, spot on middle stump, and the batter was a year and a half too late coming down on it. The ball hit the base of the leg stump.

Jack Grylls then swung everything at the next four balls and missed them all.

Erica had the final over. A lucky inside edge went for two. The next ball was straight and hit the batter's front pad . . . and something amazing happened. Herr Dryer gave him out lbw. Frankie pretended to faint.

Dean Caroota came in. "Watch out for that umpire, mate," said Frankie. "He's trigger happy . . . and he's just changed sides."

Deano ignored him and cracked a four over square-leg from the last ball of the innings. Immediately it started raining again. They'd scored 102 for nine from their 25 overs.

"Lovely weather for Duckworth-Lewis," said Tylan as we walked off in the rain.

HOME TEAM	G.LORY GARDENS v WOOLAGONG	AWAY TEAM	AT GLORY GARDENS. DATE JULY 29TH.

INNINGS OF WOOLAGONG	TOSS WON BY W.'SONG WEATHER WET

BATSMAN	RUNS SCORED	HOW OUT	BOWLER	SCORE
1 D. HOLDRIGHT	1·2·3	c̶t̶ SEBASTIEN	JOHANSEN	6
2 I. SUSZ	·1·1·2·1	c̶t̶ DA COSTA	JOHANSEN	5
3 R GONZALES	1·4·1·1·2·4·2·2·2·2·4·2·4·1·2 1·2	st ALLEN	DAVIES	37
4 G. KYNASTON	1·4·2·3·2	c & b	SEBASTIEN	12
5 T. STACHIEWITZ	4·2·1·2	bowled	KNIGHT	9
6 D. FITCH	1·1·1·2	c̶t̶ ALLEN	KNIGHT	5
7 D. VAUGHAN	2	lbw	DAVIES	2
8 M. SQUIRRELL		bowled	DAVIES	0
9 S. BANNERJEE	1·4	bowled	WOOF	5
10 J. GRYLLS		NOT	OUT	0
11 D. CAROOTA	4·	NOT	OUT	4

FALL OF WICKETS										BYES	1·2·1·2·1·2	9	TOTAL EXTRAS	17
SCORE	13	14	59	68	91	91	96	98		10	L.BYES	1·2·2	5	TOTAL	102
											WIDES	1·1	2	FOR	
BAT NO	1	2	4	5	6	3	8	9	7		NO BALLS	1	1	WKTS	9

SCORE AT A GLANCE

BOWLER	BOWLING ANALYSIS ⊙ NO BALL + WIDE													OVS	MDS	RUNS	WKT
	1	2	3	4	5	6	7	8	9	10	11	12	13				
1 B. WOOF	:2:	:1	⊠	ᴺᴮ W:	⊠									3	0	8	1
2 J. GUNN	:1	:3: 2	:4:	M	M	⊠								5	2	11	0
3 K. JOHANSEN	ᵂ1: 2	:1:	:4:	⊠										3	0	12	2
4 T. VELLACOTT	2· : ·2:	:2·0 :2:	·?	⊠										2	0	16	0
5 H. KNIGHT	:2:	:2: 2:	W2:	·: 2W	⊠									5	0	12	2
6 C. SEBASTIEN	:W:	·2:	:1: 4	⊠										3	0	18	1
7 E. DAVIES	:1:	·:	:W· W: 2·4											4	0	11	3
8																	
9																	

Chapter Nine

The shower didn't last very long but we began our innings in the worst light of the day. If Cal and Matthew had forgotten how fast the Woolagong opening bowlers were, they soon got uncomfortable reminders. Matthew was hit just above the thigh pad by a nasty lifter from Jack Grylls and Cal took a rising ball on the glove and it deflected into his ribs. Caroota was growling at the batters and straining a bit too hard for pace, and several deliveries were sprayed down the leg side. He gave away seven wides in his first two overs.

"It's lucky old Jim's umpiring at the top end," said Jacky. "I don't suppose Herr Dryer would have given us any extras."

Without Azzie, who still hadn't showed up, our batting looked more fragile than ever. It was so important for the openers to give us a good start. Cal and Matt played carefully, picking off the short singles where they could and running well between the wickets. The target wasn't enormous – roughly four an over – but the light was bad and the outfield slow because of the rain. Thanks to the wides, though, we were very nearly up with the asking rate after six overs. Then Robbie Gonzales made a double change. As expected he bowled Si Bannerjee from the bottom end, but the bowler from the top, a seamer, was new to us – he hadn't appeared in either of the first two games. He came off a long run, almost as long as Dean Caroota's, but there was none of Dean's flowing rhythm as he approached the crease; all the power came from his shoulders. His first ball was genuinely quick, though. It surprised Cal and caught him halfway up his pads going back onto the stumps. A glance at the umpire was enough to tell Cal what he already knew. He was out.

Clive strode out to the middle in his usual catlike way and glanced his first ball for a leisurely two runs.

"There's something funny about that guy's bowling," said Cal, settling down alongside us to take off his pads. "Watch his arm action. See?"

The seamer stuttered in the bowling stride and launched the ball at Clive. "You're right, it's a chuck," said Marty. "You can see his arm straighten. He's throwing it."

If the bowling arm straightens at the point of delivery, then it is an illegal action and the bowler can be no-balled for throwing. The question is whether the bowler's arm begins the action bent and then straightens. If it remains bent throughout the delivery is fair.

"Nothing surprising about that," said Jacky. "They've got a bent umpire, a bent scorer, and now a bent-armed bowler."

"It's the square-leg umpire's job to no-ball him. But old Jim's not even looking," said Cal.

"Someone ought to tell him," said Jacky. "I will if you like."

"Better not," I said.

Clive seemed to be taking control when the chucker, who, Jo informed us, was called Darrell Vaughan, suddenly found a yard of extra pace and Clive played the ball a bit away from his body and snicked it to the keeper. Then Si got a quicker delivery to bounce awkwardly on Matthew, who gloved an easy chance to slip.

I joined Erica in the middle, only too aware that we were the last two specialist batters before the long tail began. We watched the scoreboard notch up 30 for three.

"Look out for the bowler at the top end," said Erica. "That funny action of his makes it hard to pick his quicker ball. Si's turning it a long way, too. Good luck."

I got off the mark, sweeping Si Bannerjee down to fine-leg for two. Then I faced the chucker for the first time. There seemed to be a lot of wrist as well as elbow in his action – like a baseball throw – and occasionally the ball would swing unpredictably. I edged just wide of the diving slip and was quite happy to get down the other end for a break and leave him to Erica. The sky was getting darker and darker and it got harder to pick the seamer's length, but we survived and the score mounted gradually 40 . . . 45 . . . 50.

The half-century mark was reached with my best shot so far; a well-timed pull forward of square. I got right on top of the ball and it came off the bat as if it has been fired out of a cannon. But the next ball was a brute of an in-swinging yorker and I picked it far too late. It hit me on the side of the boot and it deflected onto the middle stump. I was furious with myself for not getting forward to it. We'd now lost four wickets, and we were less than halfway to our target.

As the light got poorer Frankie played like a whirling dervish. He flailed away at his first two balls from the spinner without getting close. Third time lucky – he connected magnificently and flat batted for six just to the right of the pavilion. The next was a dreadful miscue which went miles in the air and was badly dropped by the fielder at deep square-leg – probably because he could hardly see it in the gloom. And then, just as the rain came down, we lost our fifth wicket. Erica tried to flick a single down the leg side and got a leading edge which flew in the air to mid-on. The Woolagong fielders rushed off congratulating each other. We were 60 for five after 16 overs.

"If we stop now we lose by three runs," Jo told me.

"But why? That doesn't make sense." I looked helplessly at the scoreboard for some sort of answer to the puzzle.

"I could tell you, but you wouldn't understand," Jo said dismissively. "All you need to know is that the Duckworth-Lewis par score for 16 overs and five wickets is 63."

"You mean they've now scored 63 instead of 102?" asked Tylan.

"Sort of."

"Outrageous. And still more outrageous," Tylan sighed.

"And what happens if the rain stops and we bat again?" I asked. "Does that mean we've only got to score four more runs to win?"

"No, stupid. If we play the full 25 overs we've still got to get 103 for victory. But if the umpires decide overs have been lost then they'll set a revised target."

I was getting more and more lost. "And what if we play again and it pours down after two overs?"

"Then the calculation depends on how many wickets are left and how many overs are lost, like I told you," Jo said, getting impatient with me.

"So how will we know whether we're winning or not?"

"I'll tell you. I'll put the revised score up at the bottom of the scoreboard at the end of each over. That'll show the batters whether they're behind or ahead of the rate."

"I give up," said Frankie. "It's like something Ohbert invented."

"Rubbish," Jo said crossly. "It's a brilliant system. Anyone with half a brain can see that."

The shower blew over and Frankie made his way out to the wicket again, this time accompanied by Kris. By now it was nearly eight o'clock and the light which had been bad was getting much worse. In spite of Jo's grumbles that they didn't understand the rules, the umpires had decided that there was time to play the full 25 overs, so no overs were deducted. Jo said that favoured Woolagong because we'd have to bat in the dark.

As we all expected, Robbie brought back his quicks to open the new session.

Dean Caroota coming out of the trees on a dark evening wasn't a proposition that even a good batter would relish. But one-eyed Frankie showed no fear. He launched all of his ample weight at every ball and connected just once in the over. That was enough to send the ball spiralling away down to the third-man boundary for four. There were two wides as well, so the total rose to 66.

"We're level now," Jo announced, leaning out of the scorebox window. "The par score's 66." Sepo wandered out like a zombie and hung two 6s on the hooks at the bottom of the scoreboard. He was looking completely bemused and had long given up the pretence of trying to score. The Duckworth-Lewis method seemed to have fused his brain.

Kris only managed two from the next over. It was all she could do to survive against Jack Grylls's searching accuracy and pace. But Frankie fended and flashed at the other end and somehow fashioned seven runs out of it. For not the first time on tour, Deano was glaring at the batter. He hated batsmen, particularly when all the luck seemed to be going their way. The score leapt up to 75 and Jo announced that we had gone ahead by two.

"Pray for rain," Marty said gloomily. "I can't see Frankie lasting much longer."

Sadly, Marty was right. Frankie's off-stump went flying as he played another head-in-the-air heave.

"Blast," Jo cried suddenly, looking up from her frantic calculations. "Here comes the rain and we're one behind now. That wicket cost us three runs."

Tylan didn't ask for instructions; if nothing else was clear he knew that we needed quick runs. He took guard and blinked into the wet and the gloom and watched Jack Grylls come tearing in towards him. He managed to deflect a fast, rising ball off his glove and the keeper chased after it, but couldn't stop the single. So far the rain was not much more than a drizzle; not enough to stop play. Kris blocked for two balls and then launched herself at the last delivery of Jack Grylls's spell. It flew between the covers and beat the despairing dive of the fielder on the boundary, who slid along on the wet grass and clattered into one of the sodden OBA.

"Four," shouted Cal. "Are we winning now, Jo?" As he spoke the rain started to come down harder and we had to run into the pavilion for shelter. Surely they'd come off now.

Jo did another calculation. "We're two ahead," she screamed excitedly from the scorebox. "80 for six."

It was now pouring. "They've got to stop. You can't play cricket in this," said Jacky.

We peered out of the windows of the pavilion watching the umpires deliberating. They decided to begin another over . . . or at least Herr Dryer did. He marched determinedly to the bowler's end and shouted, "Play."

"He'll be needing a hair dryer after this," said Cal.

"Why doesn't he bring them off?" asked Azzie.

"Obvious, isn't it?" sneered Jacky, who was padded up to go in next.

There was a change of bowler at the top end. Both Grylls and Caroota had come to the end of their spells and George Kynaston was brought on. Robbie lost no time, he didn't even bother to reset the field. We watched George turn at the end of his run-up, race in and bowl to Tylan. Tylan shuffled forward from the crease and was hit on the front pad. There was an enormous appeal all round the ground and the umpire's finger shot up. Then as Tylan walked off, soaked to the skin, Herr Dryer looked up at the skies, glanced over towards Jim Davy and took off the bails.

"Outrageous," muttered Cal, doing a Tylan impersonation.

"Told you so," said Jacky. "He'd have given that lb if it had hit Ty on the helmet."

Jo stormed into the pavilion, her scorebook in her hand. "You know what he's done, that umpire? He's handed them the match – simple as that. Tylan's dismissal means we lose by one run."

The Woolagong players burst in out of the rain and the victory congratulations began immediately. George Kynaston got an extra big cheer for taking the final wicket. But it had been Chucker Vaughan's three for 15 from five overs that had won them the game and the series.

"Three cheers for the chucker," Jacky said, his voice dripping with sarcasm. "And an extra loud cheer for match-fixer Dryer."

I eventually shook hands with Robbie. "Well played," he said. "You nearly pulled it off, mate, but not quite. I think 2–1 was a fair reflection in the end, don't you?"

I could scarcely be bothered to reply.

We didn't hang around for long after the game. As I left the last thing I saw was Robbie and his team, jumping up and down in front of the TV camera, celebrating their hollow victory.

INNINGS OF GLORY GARDENS | TOSS WON BY W'GONG WEATHER W.E.T.

BATSMAN	RUNS SCORED	HOW OUT	BOWLER	SCORE
1 M. ROSE	6·1·1·1·2 >>	ct SUSZ	BANNERJEE	7
2 C. SEBASTIEN	1·1·2·1·1 >>	lbw	VAUGHAN	6
3 C. DA COSTA	2·1·3·2 >>	ct SQUIRRELL	VAUGHAN	8
4 E. DAVIES	2·1·1·1 >>	ct HOLDRIGHT	BANNERJEE	5
5 H. KNIGHT	2·1·2·2·4 >>	bowled	VAUGHAN	11
6 F. ALLEN	6·3·4·3·2 >>	bowled	GRYLLS	18
7 K. JOHANSEN	2·1·4	NOT	OUT	7
8 T. VELLACOTT	1 >>	lbw	KYNASTON	1
9 J. GUNN				
10 B. WOOF				
11 P. BENNETT				

FALL OF WICKETS

	1	2	3	4	5	6	7	8	9	10
SCORE	20	28	30	50	60	75	80			
BAT NO	2	3	1	5	4	6	8			

BYES	2·	2
L.BYES	1·1·1	3
WIDES	1·1·4·2·1	10
NO BALLS	1·1	2

TOTAL EXTRAS 17
TOTAL 80
TOTAL FOR 7 WKTS

SCORE AT A GLANCE

BOWLING ANALYSIS ⊙ NO BALL   + WIDE

BOWLER	1	2	3	4	5	6	7	8	9	10	11	12	13	OVS	MDS	RUNS	WKT
1 D. CARDOTA				X	X									5	0	24	0
2 J. GRYLLS					X									5	0	15	1
3 D. VAUGHAN					X									5	0	15	3
4 S. BANNERJEE					X									5	0	21	2
5 G. KYNASTON														0·1	0	0	1
6																	
7																	
8																	
9																	

Chapter Ten

Next morning the phone rang and it was Kiddo. He sounded irritable.

"Where have you been, kiddo?"

"Here. In my bedroom."

"Then why didn't you answer the phone?"

"I was asleep."

"It's 11 o'clock, for crissake. I've been calling you all morning. And I want to know whether any of you lot have been sounding off to the media."

"You mean that TV reporter?"

"Him or the newspapers. I've had the *Gazette* on this morning – a pushy young journalist. She was asking questions about yesterday's game. 'Match fixing' were the words she used, would you believe. I want to know who's been putting about silly stories like that."

"Well, it wasn't me."

"I hope not. Did any of you talk to that TV reporter yesterday?"

"No. They didn't want to do an interview this time. Not with me anyway."

"Well someone must have started it. I hope it wasn't Walter Whitman after a bit of extra publicity."

"I don't think he'd do that."

"Nor do I. But I'm not having a kids' cricket competition turned into a bloomin' Body-line Series."

"What's a Body-line Series?"

"It was when England played in Australia, years ago. The Australians said our bowlers were cheating."

"Were they?"

"The bowlers weren't. They were under instructions to bowl bouncers to a leg-side field and they were good at it, especially Harold Larwood. He must have been one of the fastest of all time."

"And we won the Ashes?"

"Yes. What did you think of yesterday's result?"

"Not much."

"A bit of a nonsense, I thought. It was a strange idea of those umpires to use the Duckworth-Lewis method at this level of cricket.

"Jo really rates it. She says it's the fairest way by far, only the umpires didn't understand it properly."

"More than likely."

"But . . . was their umpire . . .?"

"Cheating? I doubt it. He may have made a decision or two which were . . . a bit partisan, in the heat of the moment. But it won't do any good to moan about it, kiddo. You've lost the one-day series. Put that behind you and win the big game this weekend."

I told Kiddo about our quiz night with Woolagong and he was pleased with the idea. He said we should hold it at the Priory on Friday night after the first day of Ohbert's Ashes.

"We'll make it a charity fundraising evening. Perhaps our friends from the press will write something nice about us for a change, if they're not too busy with their match-fixing theories."

He rang off.

Last night's game had left the whole team feeling flat and demotivated. It was my job to pick them up again in time for Ohbert's Ashes. But how? I felt confused myself about the way the game had finished. It didn't seem fair. And if cricket wasn't played honestly there wasn't much point in playing it at all.

As usual when I wasn't sure what to do next I went to talk to Cal about it – it's very handy having my best friend living next door. Unfortunately Mack came too, he was still silently following me about. When we arrived we found Frankie there as well. He showed us his black eye; it was amazing close up: purple, yellow, red, brown – every colour you can think of, except black.

Frankie was having a moan about Jo, which was nothing new. "She's gone cricket quiz mad, my sister," he said. "She never stops asking me stupid questions, such as: Who was the heaviest cricketer to play for England?"

"Who was it?" I asked.

"I can't remember."

"Probably W. G. Grace," Mack said suddenly. They were the first words he'd spoken all day.

"Yeah, that's him."

"Name the top England fast bowler in the Body-line Series." I said.

"Don't you start," protested Frankie.

"It was Harold Larwood," said Mack

Frankie looked at me. "Is he right?" I nodded. "Fantastic. You've got to be in the quiz team, Mack."

"I don't want to be," said Mack sullenly.

"Why not?"

"Because . . . I don't. Okay?" Mack sat down and stared into the distance.

"Okay, suit yourself," said Frankie. "We'll still win with Azzie in the team."

"Have you heard from him?" I asked.

"Yeah, he rang Jo this morning. His little brother ran away from home just before the game started and the whole family was out looking for him. They even called the police. They found him late last night watching TV round one of his mates. You can imagine how pleased Azzie was to miss the game, particularly when Jo told him we'd lost."

I told them about Kiddo's phone call and neither Cal nor Frankie seemed a bit surprised.

"I think Jacky might have said something after the game," said Cal. "He's very excited about this cheating thing."

"I thought his head was going to do a volcanic eruption," said Frankie.

"He's getting the whole thing out of focus," said Cal. "So what if we've had a few bad umpiring decisions and their scorer can't add up. It's not the end of life on earth, is it?"

"It's not the end of the story, either," Mack said quietly. We all turned and looked at him. Slowly he pulled a piece of paper out of his pocket and handed it to me to read:

> *Dear Traitor,*
>   *That's what we call an Aussie who plays for a pom team. We don't like poms, but traitors are worse. If you play again, watch out. Your pommy friends won't be able to help you.*
>   *Ned Kelly*

"Who's Ned Kelly?" asked Frankie.

"He's a famous Australian outlaw," said Mack.

"Like Billy the Kid?"

"Sort of."

"What's he doing in England, then?"

"He's not, you thicko. Ned Kelly's dead. It's a whatsits-name."

"Pseudonym," said Cal. "Where did the letter come from?"

"I found it on my bag in the changing room after the first game. I should have tossed it in the bin but . . ."

"Why didn't you tell us sooner?" asked Cal.

"Because . . . maybe I should have, but I didn't want to whinge about it."

"Who sent it? Any idea?" I asked.

"Must be a real sicko," said Frankie.

"It seems obvious to me. It has to be one of the Woolagong gang."

"You ought to show it to Kiddo," I said.

"No way."

"We should find out who sent it. Do a handwriting test or something," said Frankie.

"Forget it, Frankie. I don't care who wrote it."

"Then what are you going to do? Just get more and more miserable?" Cal asked impatiently.

"No. I've just made up my mind about it, this minute. That's why I showed you the letter. If I'm picked, I'm going to play in the Ashes game. And I'll do everything I can to help Glory Gardens win. If anyone thinks that makes me a traitor, they can barbecue their head."

"Sounds just like an Aussie bloke called Mack McCurdy, I once knew," said Frankie slapping him on the back. "Don't get mad, get even."

"If we're going to beat them, we'll need a plan," said Cal.

"What sort of plan?" asked Frankie. "Kidnap Herr Dryer? Poison the burgers at the barbecue? I know – we could send Ohbert's Barmy Army round to keep them awake all week. Or, better still, Ohbert could go at dead of night and smoke them out of their rooms."

"I mean a cricket plan, fathead. We've got to decide on how to build an innings and how to bowl at them – and stick to it. We've never played a three-day game before and it's going to be really tough."

"And I'll give everyone sledging lessons, too," said Frankie. "Their captain didn't like a dose of his own medicine much, did he?"

"Take care, Frankie. We don't want Herr Dryer sending you off," I said.

"Tylan thinks he's an alien trying to start the Third World War," said Frankie.

"That explains why he's disguised as Adolf Hitler," said Mack.

"Yeah, Hitler comes back and starts World War Three at the Priory, starting with Australia declaring war on England – and you'll get thrown in a prisoner-of-war camp, Mack, because you're an Aussie."

"No, I'm not, I'm a pom double agent," said Mack, laughing for the first time in a week.

"Does that mean you'll change your mind about being in the quiz team, too?" asked Frankie

"Why not?"

"Then watch out, Ned Kelly, Mad Mack McCurdy's on your tail."

Picking the team for Ohbert's Ashes was never going to be easy. Marty was fit again and Jo insisted that Ohbert had to play. "We don't play Ohbert's Ashes without Ohbert," she said firmly. In the end we agreed on a selection of 12 players:

Matthew Rose	Mack McCurdy
Cal Sebastien	Frankie Allen
Azzie Nazar	Tylan Vellacott
Clive da Costa	Jacky Gunn
Erica Davies	Marty Lear
Hooker Knight	Ohbert Bennett

The final decision on which one to leave out was left to me to make on the morning f the game, after I'd had a good look at the pitch.

The most likely candidates for twelfth man, if we had to play Ohbert, were Tylan, Mack or Matthew. I was keen to have Tylan in the team to provide us with the variety we needed against their top batters such as Robbie, George and Dai Holdright, especially since it was a three-day game. Matthew was just the sort of defensive player you needed to stick around in a two-innings match, too. That left Mack. His fielding was worth twenty or thirty runs, not to mention the inspiration he brought to the others. And I was worried in case the disappointment of not playing cast him back into the gloom again. It wasn't going to be an easy decision.

On Thursday, the day before the big game, the *Gazette* came out. There was a big picture of Wally shaking hands with Robbie after the game under a headline which said: SMOULDERING ASHES.

The report was only short, but it was poisonous. I saw immediately what Kiddo had been worrying about:

The local young cricketers of Glory Gardens C.C. were beaten 2–1 by their Australian challengers, Woolagong C.C., in a closely fought one-day series which finished at the weekend. Woolagong's captain, Robbie Gonzales, being congratulated here by Walter Whitman, chairman of Whitmart, said, "It was a tough, competitive tournament and we're very happy to have come out on top. When the going gets tough, the toughs get going, as Shane Warne says."

But the new generation of cricketers seem to be learning more than just competitive spirit from their heroes. There was talk of illegal bowling, corrupt umpiring and even match fixing after Sunday's game. Friday sees the first day of a three-day match at the Whitmart Priory between the two young teams. We hope the Junior Ashes will be played in the right spirit – like the good and simple game cricket always used to be.

Chapter Eleven

On Friday morning the sun was shining. There had been a lot of rain in the week and Bunter, the Priory groundsman, said the pitch would be a bit lively first thing and then get better and better. If I won the toss I thought I'd probably put them in and opt for a run chase.

There had been good news and bad news the previous evening at nets. First I'd watched Marty bowling flat out and looking as if he was right back in the groove. That was a big bonus. But then Clive told me that he wasn't going to be able to play. Clive's never been the most reliable member of the team, but this time it wasn't his fault. His aunt had just been offered a free, week's holiday for two in Spain, leaving on Saturday morning and she'd told Clive she wouldn't go without him. Clive knew she'd be terribly disappointed if they didn't go – though not much more disappointed than he was at missing the game. He said he'd come along and coach us on Friday and ring from Spain on Sunday night to get the result.

The loss of one of our top two batters was a dreadful blow, but at least I didn't have to tell Mack he was twelfth man. It was a tragedy for Frankie, who had been looking forward to three days of chocolate brownies for lunch and tea.

"You'd think his aunt would be more thoughtful than to go away at such an important time for the club," he moaned.

As we walked out to the middle, Robbie wasted no time in letting me know that he'd seen the article in the *Gazette*.

"You'd better toss, mate," he said dryly. "I don't want to be accused of using a double-headed coin."

I pretended not to understand and, after another look at the pitch, I spun my 50p. He called "Tails" – and he got it right. "Then I guess you can bat first," said Robbie. "And by the way, if you think the bowling's illegal, let me know, won't you? I'll call the cops and have the lot of them arrested." He stalked off. I caught up with him again but I didn't know what to say.

"You coming to the quiz tonight?" I said lamely. Jo had arranged it for half past seven in the pavilion and she was expecting a big audience.

"Yeah, we'll be there," said Robbie. "We've got Si, Gryllsy and Sepo on our team. I reckon they'll be good enough for you, even without cheating."

"Listen," I said. "I didn't write that stuff in the paper."

"Someone fed them the lines, though, didn't they?"

"I don't know who it was, *and* I think it's a complete load of rubbish."

"If you say so." He turned and looked at me, narrowing his eyes. "May the best team win and the losers take it on the chin," he said. We shook hands on that.

The only good thing about the piece in the *Gazette* was the size of the crowd. It seemed that half the old-age pensioners in town had come along to watch the fun. I'd never seen so many deckchairs. The OBA were at the canal end. Whatever the appeal was of dressing up like Ohbert, it was definitely catching on. There were nine or ten of them here today and they were holding a big banner which read, puzzlingly, OHBERT FOR PRESIDENT!

Wally Whitman came and wished us good luck before the game started. "I've got a surprise lined up for you lot on Sunday," he said. "Someone you all know is coming to present the prizes. So you'd better win."

"Who? Is it someone famous?" asked Frankie.

"Wait and see. Do you have a trophy for this game?"

We all looked at Ohbert, who wasn't listening.

"A trophy, Ohbert? Do we have one?" Frankie said, removing Ohbert's headset and shouting into his ear.

"Oh but . . . yes. It's a secret, though."

Wally nodded solemnly. "Then we'll need a secret arrangement for picking it up, won't we. Tell you what. Here's my spare mobile. I'll call you later to fix things up."

Ohbert took the mobile phone and inspected it with growing pleasure. A big grin spread slowly across his face. "Oh but . . . can I use it?"

"Of course you can," said Wally.

"Why do you want a phone, Ohbert? You don't know anyone," said Frankie.

"Take no notice, Ohbert – he only does it to annoy," Jo said, with a stern look at her brother.

Sid Burns, our regular umpire, was back on duty, and he and Herr Dryer led the Woolagong players out on to the pitch to a ripple of applause and shouts of "Ohbert! Ohbert!" from the canal end. The TV cameraman was already in action by the pavilion and Kiddo was having a very serious conversation with the red-faced reporter.

Cal and Matthew received a warm ovation as they walked out together. Frankie shouted, "See you both at lunch time." There was a quiet buzz of anticipation round the ground which turned to complete silence as Dean Caroota ran in to bowl the first ball of Ohbert's Ashes. It was quick and bounced just outside the off-stump, and Matthew let it go.

"He's fired up this morning, I can tell," said Marty. He was right. Dean was soon bowling a yard faster than at any time on the entire tour and Matthew didn't know how to handle the extra pace. It took him several overs to hit anything in the middle of the bat. Nevertheless, Cal's was the first wicket to fall, in Dean Caroota's third over. With the score on 7, he got a fine outside edge through to the keeper.

Azzie opened his account with two cracking fours off Jack Grylls and then he started to attack Caroota, too. A fierce pull flew to the boundary and hit the rope so hard that it bounced over the heads of some old spectators in their deckchairs. Then a delicate leg glide gave him three more. At the other end Matthew was defending as only Matthew can. His forward defensive is straight out of the textbook and when he plays back, everything is behind the ball.

Azzie plays the pull shot early and on the front foot. His head is over the ball and he rolls his wrists on contact to keep it down. Notice the balance and position of his feet. The shot is completely under control.

Frankie, sitting next to me, yawned loudly, but, for a change, he didn't complain about Matt's slow scoring. Even Frankie understood the importance of occupying the crease at this stage of the game. As long as Azzie was striking the ball hard at the other end, we had the perfect combination of attack and defence.

Azzie was badly dropped at mid-on miscuing a drive, but he continued to go for his shots, hitting out with astonishing power.

He took seven and six off successive overs from Dean Caroota and Robbie was forced to rest his fast bowler. Si Bannerjee's leg-spin regained some control, but whenever a bad ball came along Azzie gave it the treatment. A front-foot pull against Jack Grylls was the shot of the morning. It was hit so hard that, although it was within diving range of mid-wicket, the fielder didn't even move. The ball rocketed past him to the boundary.

The 50 came up in the fifteenth over. "Matthew: 5; Azzie: 35," said Frankie gleefully. "Az has forgotten it's a three-dayer and Matthew thinks we're playing for a five-day draw."

For three overs Matt kept the strike and the runs virtually dried up. Then Azzie was back in action, driving both bowlers through extra cover for two more glorious boundaries.

It was a dream start, particularly after losing the early wicket. I imagined how Robbie would be feeling about putting us in, as he watched Azzie hammering his bowlers out of the ground. The score rolled on steadily to 70 for one and it seemed that nothing could stop our progress. Frankie thought so. He was crowing happily about sending Woolagong packing with the worst hammering in their history.

"They haven't even got Chucker Vaughan playing for them today," he said, spotting the bowler walking round the boundary to take Jack Grylls a drink between overs. "They must be scared that old Sid will no-ball him."

Sid Burns was officiating from the top end today and Herr Dryer was at the canal end from where Si was bowling up the hill. So far, at least, there hadn't been a single appeal for him to get wrong.

"Azzie's on 48," shouted Jo.

He was on strike too, facing Cameron Armstrong and, even before Jo put his score up on the board, you could tell that he knew exactly how many he'd got from the slightly edgy way he was looking for runs. Twice Matthew sent him back as he darted down the pitch for a suicide single. Then he received a short one, wide of the off-stump, and cut hard. The boundary fielder raced round and kept the scoring down to two, but it was enough to bring up the half-century. I couldn't remember when I'd seen a better one. Even Clive's great knock in the second one-dayer wasn't in this class. Azzie waved his bat at us and Frankie and the OBA led the congratulations. It must have been a bit odd for Azzie to hear his half-century acclaimed by a loud chant of "Ohbert! Ohbert!"

The crowd was even bigger now. Wally gave us a wave and a thumbs up. He had moved his umbrella from his usual position at the bottom end to the other side of the ground, probably to get as far away from the OBA as possible.

The celebrations ended and Azzie settled again to face Armstrong. It was another widish delivery and, trying to repeat the cut shot, Azzie dragged it straight into the base of his off-stump.

"Oh but . . . is he out?" asked Ohbert, looking up from playing with the buttons of Wally's mobile to see Azzie walking back.

"Well done, Ohbert. Keep up the commentary," said Cal.

Erica was already on her way to the wicket. "72 for two. Lunch next target," I shouted.

Azzie had hit seven fours in his 50 which had come from just 48 balls. After that anything – particularly the sight of Matthew and Erica accumulating their runs at less than two an over – was bound to be an anticlimax. But I was happy with the way things were going, until, just as it looked as if we'd come in at the break with only two wickets down in the session, Erica flicked at one down the leg side which bounced on her more than she expected and she gloved it to the keeper. It was the last ball before lunch and we came in at 85 for three.

"That's a new one for the *Guiness Book of Records*. Matt's scored fifteen singles in 33 overs," Frankie shouted as Matthew came up the steps of the pavilion.

Erica stood back and let him take the applause. She looked very downcast. "Sorry, Hooker," she said. "That was a terrible shot to play just before lunch. I can't think why I did it."

"That's okay," I mumbled, but she was right, the loss of her wicket had brought Woolagong firmly back into the game.

During lunch a jazz band appeared and played to the crowd while they ate their picnics. "That's another Wally idea," said Frankie. "He likes jazz and they're coming tomorrow and Sunday, too."

"Wally ideas, right," said Tylan, who wasn't impressed with the music.

"Oh but, I like them," Ohbert said, nodding his head to the music as he fiddled happily with the text display on his new mobile.

To get my concentration going for batting after lunch, I tried to have a couple of moments alone in the changing room before I went out, but Frankie came in and wrecked that plan.

"How many do we need, Hook?" he asked.

"At least 200," I said. "I'd like to make 250."

"Easy-peasy," he said. "The stage is set for a Frankie Allen 50. I feel a master innings coming on today." I left Frankie to his dreams and joined Matthew who was waiting to walk out to the middle.

"Just keep it going," I said to Matt. "If you're still there on 30 at tea, we'll be happy."

I watched Robbie set a field for Dean Caroota, who was returning at the top end, and I still can't believe that I didn't spot his plan. It was so obvious. Deano ran in and bowled a bouncer on leg stump and I hooked instinctively. As I played the shot I realised I'd fallen for the oldest trick in the book. The ball took a top edge and the squarer of the two fielders at backward square leg ran in and took a straightforward catch.

"Goodnight, sucker," said a delighted Dean Caroota. The rest of the team rushed up to him, and I walked away from the jeers and the high-fives. I was furious with myself. Back in the pavilion I slammed the dressing room door to let everyone know I didn't want to be disturbed. It took me a good fifteen minutes to calm down. I emerged again just in time to see Matthew going down the wicket to Si Bannerjee and planting him over mid-on for four.

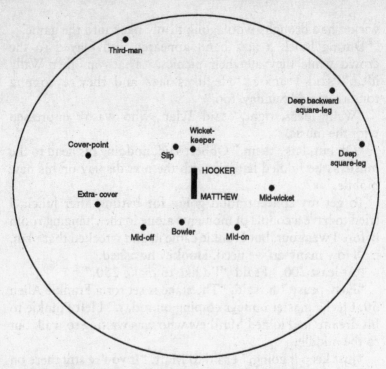

The two deep fielders on the leg side are positioned deliberately for the ball hooked in the air.

"You're missing Matt the Magnificent," shouted Frankie to me. "It was all singles before lunch but it's been boundaries ever since. That's his fourth four since the restart."

"Two of them were streaky edges through the slips," said Marty.

"Don't forget the back-foot drive. That was a class shot," said Erica.

The score had rolled on to 107 for four and Matthew and Mack had put on a mini partnership of 22 since my dismissal. But, just as I was beginning to get over my own sad contribution, Matthew went back on his stumps to pull Si and missed completely. It would have been a big surprise if Herr Dryer hadn't given the lbw decision against him, but when the finger went up Jacky couldn't resist another moan. "There it goes again. The fastest digit in the West."

Dean Caroota bowled to Frankie – it was the first ball he had received. He heaved and missed, and looked back at the wreckage of his stumps.

"Bring on another sucker," Dean shouted aggressively.

Tylan lasted two balls more than Frankie before padding up to a straight one. Three wickets had fallen on 107 and, with seven now down, we were suddenly in a big, big hole. Mack tried to restore calm, but Jacky's batting against Bannerjee's spin didn't inspire any confidence at all. Sure enough, it wasn't long before he was given out lbw. But Jacky stood his ground and glared at the Woolagong umpire. "I hit that," he shouted angrily.

Matthew uses his feet against the spinner to get to the pitch of the ball. Giving himself room, he hits with the spin over mid-off.

"I know you did. After it hit your pad," said Herr Dryer, coldly, "You're out, boy."

Jacky didn't move for a full five seconds. Then, with a snort of disbelief, he turned his back on umpire and bowler and made his exit. We'd now registered four ducks since lunch in a collapse which had gone from 85 for three to 112 for eight.

Jacky was too angry to speak, which was just as well, because Kiddo was sitting with us and I knew he wasn't at all impressed about the way the umpire's decision had been challenged. The ninth wicket fell on 118 – Marty played miles away from his body and offered a regulation snick to the keeper.

And so, finally, Ohbert emerged from the pavilion to do battle. He had transformed himself into a cross between the Michelin Man and an ice-hockey goalkeeper. He was covered from head to foot in body armour: helmet, visor, forearm shields, and he must have been wearing the whole team's collection of thigh pads and chest protectors. The OBA didn't recognise him at first – then the biggest cheer of the day rose from the canal end. Ohbert waddled comically towards the wicket. With all that padding and armour, it seemed unlikely that he'd ever be able to run from one end of the pitch to the other. But Ohbert didn't care; he was in casual mood today. He took some sort of guard and then wobbled down the pitch for a chat with Mack, who sent him back and told him to get on with it.

He nearly ran himself out first ball, and Mack, second ball. But somehow he survived Si's spin and stood fidgeting at the non-striker's end as Dean Caroota ran in. The fast bowler was just approaching the stumps when there was a sudden, very loud, burst of electronic music. He nearly fell over, shuddered to a stop and stared angrily in Ohbert's direction. The tune continued; it sounded like "Jingle Bells". Ohbert appeared confused and then started searching vaguely for something in his pockets. At last, with some difficulty, he pulled out Wally's mobile phone, put it to his ear and listened. After a pause, he handed the phone to Dean. "It's for you," he said.

Dean Caroota grabbed the phone with a look of both anger and puzzlement. As he listened his eyes grew wider and wider. It was just then that I noticed Frankie on the steps of the pavilion speaking into another mobile. When he saw me he started to splutter with laughter. "Just a bit of one-to-one sledging," he managed to gasp eventually. "I thought Deano needed some personal training."

Without a smile Herr Dryer took the phone from an apoplectic Deano, switched it off and put it in his pocket. The game continued. Mack kept the strike for two overs but eventually Ohbert found himself at the bottom end facing the raging Dean Caroota. Robbie had no idea how to set a field to Ohbert but in the end he decided to bring everyone in except third-man and long-leg. Ohbert walked down the pitch to meet a lightning-fast ball from Caroota and poked his bat at it. It flew off the middle, past square-leg, for four.

The next ball was even faster and it hit Ohbert full on the toe. He threw down his bat and hopped away up the pitch on one leg. Then he rolled on his back and couldn't get up. Slim Squirrell casually picked up the ball and removed the bails.

"Oh but, am I out?" asked Ohbert as he struggled to his feet at the third attempt and saw everyone else walking off.

"You bet, mate," Deano said unsmilingly. "Run out and a nice black toe, too." We had sunk to a sad 123 all out.

HOME TEAM	GLORY GARDENS V WOOLAGONG		AWAY TEAM	AT WHITMART PRIORY DATE AUG. 4TH

INNINGS OF GLORY GARDENS | TOSS WON BY W'GONG WEATHER SUNNY

BATSMAN	RUNS SCORED	HOW OUT	BOWLER	SCORE
1 M. ROSE	1.1.1.1.1.1.1.1.1.1.1.1.1.1.4.4.4.4	lbw	BANNERJEE	31
2 C. SEBASTIEN	1.2	ct SQUIRRELL	CAROOTA	3
3 A. NAZAR	4.4.4.3.1.2.2.2.1.4.2.2.4.4.1 4.1.(4.5)2.1.2	bowled	ARMSTRONG	50
4 E. DAVIES	2.1.2	ct SQUIRRELL	KYNASTON	5
5 H. KNIGHT		ct STACHIEWITZ	CAROOTA	0
6 T. McCURDY	1.4.1.2.1.2.1	NOT	OUT	12
7 F. ALLEN		bowled	CAROOTA	0
8 T. VELLACOTT		lbw	CAROOTA	0
9 J. GUNN		lbw	BANNERJEE	0
10 M. LEAR	1.2	ct SQUIRRELL	BANNERJEE	3
11 P. BENNETT	1.4	RUN	OUT	5

FALL OF WICKETS											BYES	1.1.1.2		6	TOTAL EXTRAS	14
SCORE	7	72	85	85	107	107	107	112	118	123	L.BYES 1.1.1.1.1			6	TOTAL FOR	123 ALL
	1	2	3	4	5	6	7	8	9	10	WIDES			1		
BAT NO	1	3	4	5	1	7	8	9	10	11	NO BALLS			1	WKTS	OUT

SCORE AT A GLANCE

BOWLING ANALYSIS ⊙ NO BALL + WIDE																
BOWLER	1	2	3	4	5	6	7	8	9	10	11	12	13	OVS	MDS	RUNS	WKT
1 D. CAROOTA							W			W				10.2	2	35	4
2 J. GRULLS	M	M							X					7	2	19	0
3 S. BANNERJEE										X				14	1	40	3
4																	
5 C. ARMSTRONG		M						M	X					8	2	12	1
6 G. KYNASTON					X									3	1	3	1
7 I. SUSZ		X												1	0	2	0
8																	
9																	

Chapter Twelve

Jacky was still seething about the unfairness of his dismissal. It was the last straw and he was looking for blood when Woolagong began their first innings.

"I wouldn't let him open from the Herr Dryer end if I were you," Cal said to me. My first instinct was not to bowl him at all until he'd calmed down and it was a pity I changed my mind.

I put him on to open at the top end where Sid Burns was umpiring; that, unfortunately, meant Marty was bowling uphill. Jacky fired his first three balls down the leg side for wides. The fourth was snicked to the keeper and Frankie dropped it. All the fury that had been building up in Jacky suddenly exploded and he let rip at Frankie. "I'm sick and tired of bowling with a fat fool who can't catch behind the stumps," he fumed. Frankie turned his back on him and pretended not to hear. The last ball of the opening over was driven to the cover boundary for four and Jacky snatched his sweater rudely from Sid Burns and stormed off to his fielding position in the deep.

Marty got a bit of movement and not much luck. Twice he was edged for boundaries and I was forced to drop out a third-man to stop the flow of runs. Frankie then put down a second chance – a much harder one this time from an inside edge. He got it in his left glove and it bounced out as his elbow hit the ground. Jacky continued from the top end but his next over wasn't much better than the first. He gave away eight runs, three of them wides and, when he finally got one in the right place, Azzie put down a difficult chance at slip.

Dropping three catches in the first three overs was hardly a dream start and, even though neither of the Woolagong openers looked very happy, particularly against Mart, the total was mounting too rapidly for comfort.

"Come on, Glory Gardens. Wake up," Clive shouted desperately from the boundary. The frustration was getting to the players, too. We badly needed a wicket.

After Jacky's third over I'd seen enough. I decided to switch Marty to the top end and come on to bowl myself at the other. Straightaway I got the ball to swing back into both right-handers and I had two good appeals for lbw in my first over. Of course Herr Dryer turned them both down, but at least he told me one of them was close. "Not doing quite enough," he said dourly. "It would have missed off-stump, but not by a lot."

At last Marty got some reward for a spell of accurate fast bowling. A nip-backer cut through Dai Holdright's groping defensive push and clipped the top of the middle stump. Dai nodded in Marty's direction to acknowledge that he'd been beaten by a beauty and then walked off.

At 47 for one, I wasn't too cheered to see Robbie Gonzales making his way confidently to the wicket.

"I'll see if I can wind him up a bit," Frankie said to me.

"Take care," I said anxiously.

"With a bit of luck you'll get yourself sent off, fatman," Cal said teasingly.

Jacky overheard him. "Good idea. Two dropped catches and five byes. Get him off before he does any more damage," he shouted unkindly.

Frankie had heard enough. "You should try keeping wicket to the rubbish you've been throwing down. The square-leg umpire had a better chance than me of stopping most of them." Jacky was in no mood for criticism. With a fist raised aggressively he rounded on Frankie. "I don't fight with people

106

who wear glasses," Frankie said coolly.

Cal and I quickly stepped between them before anything silly could happen. "Keep your energy for the opposition, both of you," I said.

Jacky skulked off to the outfield again and Frankie stuck his tongue out at him behind his back.

I adjusted my field for the left-hander with five on the leg side, including Azzie at leg-slip.

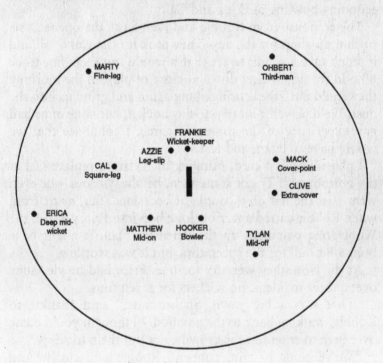

Robbie looked dangerous. Right from the start he was busy, working everything on his legs into space and never missing the chance of a run. Behind him Frankie kept up a ball-by-ball commentary mixed up with his usual nonsense. He mocked Robbie each time he played and missed, told him his socks didn't match and even asked him why, with a name like Gonzales, he wasn't a bullfighter rather than a cricketer.

It would have put off most batters, but Robbie hardly seemed to notice.

The 50 was up in the ninth over and 60 in the twelfth. At the same time as concentrating on my bowling I was wracking my brains for other ideas for getting the breakthrough. The opener drove me back over my head for four and, next over, Robbie cracked Marty's full toss into the fence. Pace and swing wasn't working, so I switched to the economy bowling of Erica and Cal.

The response from Robbie and Ivan Susz, the opener, was to shut up shop for the day. They took no chances at all and it didn't take a genius to see that it would suit them fine to be 80 odd for one wicket down at close of play. In the morning they could push the scoring along again and grind us into the dust. We'd played a lot of one-day cricket, but none of us had any experience of the three-day game. I could see that we would have to learn, and fast.

I played my last card, bringing on Tylan to replace Cal at the bottom end. Ty got some turn, he always does – he even went past the bat on a couple of occasions. But, apart from when Robbie carted a terrible long hop into Priory Road, the Woolagong pair kept up the defensive plan. It might have been a bit dull for the spectators, but it was working.

At the close they were 89 for one. Erica had bowled nine overs, three maidens, no wickets for seven runs.

"That was a big yawn, Shane mate," said Frankie to Robbie, walking back to the pavilion. "I thought you'd come over here to entertain the crowds, not put them to sleep."

"We've come to win, cobber," Robbie said curtly. And from the look in his eyes it was clear that he thought Woolagong already had the game in the bag.

The atmosphere in the pavilion afterwards was tense to say the least. Jacky told Robbie that the umpiring had been a disgrace and refused to stay for the barbecue and quiz. "I'll be up early and ready for you lot in the morning. Don't forget to say your prayers when you go to bed," he said as he left.

Matthew didn't stop either, he said he was a bit tired after his innings. That upset Jo because she'd put a lot of work into the the evening and she told Matthew she thought he was a wimp.

Not surprisingly, I was beginning to have serious doubts about whether the quiz was a good idea, but at least Frankie and Woofy were determined to enjoy themselves and they tucked heartily into the food that Wally had organised.

"Brilliant, as usual," mumbled Woofy, pushing a spare rib in the vague direction of his mouth. "It was worth coming for the food, even if the cricket was rubbish."

The barbecue didn't have a bad effect on the Woolagong players, either. Slowly the two teams began to mix and talk about the day's cricket. Even Dean Caroota was a bit more friendly when he was holding a large plate of kebabs drowned in tomato ketchup, instead of a cricket ball.

"That was good bowling," Marty said to him. "'Specially the second spell."

"Thanks," Deano said, with ketchup running down his chin. "I'm getting used to these pitches at last. They're much slower than the ones back home. You have to pitch up, but, if you do, you get a lot more sideways movement."

Si and Tylan were chatting busily about flippers and googlies and top-spinners, and Robbie was telling Ohbert about Shane Warne; it was a bad choice of audience because Ohbert was the only person in the ground who'd never heard of "Warnie". Even Mack was mixing with the Woolagong players for just about the first time since they'd arrived.

Kiddo came over to me for a quiet word. "I'm afraid they've got the upper hand, kiddo," he began.

"Yeah. We threw it away with our middle-order batting."

"There's a long way to go yet," he said reassuringly. I could see there was something else on his mind and, after a pause, he continued. "I've been talking to their manager. He tells me that they didn't play that young bowler today – what's his name? Vaughan? – because Mr Dryer thinks he's got a suspect action.

"Oh," I said, slightly surprised.

"And there's another thing – he also apologised for the shambles at the end of the last game. He said none of them, least of all the umpire, knew who had won until Jo told them. So that clears up a couple of matters, don't you think?"

"Yes," I agreed. If it was true it meant Cal was right: Herr Dryer wasn't trying to fix the results in favour of Woolagong – he was just a useless umpire. But that still didn't explain Mack's letter. Whoever had written that certainly wasn't a believer in fair play. I thought of telling Kiddo about it, but decided it was Mack's affair, not mine.

Soon it was time for the quiz. A good crowd, mostly made up of parents and Priory players, were seated in the pavilion and they gave Jo a noisy welcome when she took her place in front of them. The two teams of three were already sitting at tables to the right and left of her.

"Good evening, ladies and gentlemen, and welcome to Ohbert's Ashes Quiz Night," Jo said, in a very professional manner. "I'm Jo Allen, your quizmaster for this evening. Can I introduce, on my right, the guest team all the way from Woolagong, New South Wales: Slim Squirrell, Si Bannerjee and Sepo Bosnitch." More applause. "And on my left, the home team, Glory Gardens: Azzie Nazar, Mack McCurdy and Paul Bennett." The OBA was there in force, crowded into the back row, and at the mention of Ohbert's name they waved their caps and shouted, "Ohbert! Mastermind!"

It was Jo's idea to have Ohbert on the team. She said it was Ohbert's Ashes and Woolagong wouldn't be here without him; the fact that he wouldn't be able to contribute one sensible answer didn't seem to worry her at all.

The quiz began with three questions for each team about the rules of cricket.

"How many ways can you be out to a no-ball?" asked Jo.

The Woolagong team conferred and Slim answered. "Four.

110

Run out, handling the ball, obstructing the field and hitting the ball twice."

"Correct. For an extra point, there's one other way you can be out off a wide. What is it?"

"Stumped," said Sepo

"Correct. A batter hits the ball and strikes short-leg on the helmet. It rebounds to the keeper who catches it. Is he out?"

"No," said Sepo, without bothering to consult the others.

"Correct again, Sepo," said Jo, her admiration clearly growing with every answer.

"He's like a cricket encyclopedia," Cal whispered to me.

"He had to be good at something," I said casually, although I too was amazed at Sepo's show of knowledge.

Woolagong were 6–5 up after the first round but the Glory Gardens team bounced back and took the lead as Mack got a bonus for getting three correct answers in a row. Then it came to Ohbert's own turn.

"Who has the best test match batting average ever, Ohbert?" asked Jo.

"Oh but . . . was it Shane Warne?" said our cricket genius.

"It was Donald Bradman. His test match average was 99.94," said Sepo, gaining a bonus point and another look of respect from Jo.

She turned to Ohbert again. "Which leg-spin bowler has taken more than 300 test wickets?"

"Brian Lara," said Ohbert, confidently.

"Shane Warne," shouted Sepo.

"I think Ohbert's got all the answers, but in the wrong order," Frankie said in my ear.

The teams were level on 38 points each. Sepo and Mack were both poised to raise their arms for the last question . . . the decider.

Jo read the question. "Who scored the fastest test match century ever, in terms of balls received?"

Mack was first but he didn't look very certain about his answer. "Was it Ian Botham?" he asked hesitantly.

"No. I can offer it to the other team."

Sepo smiled. "It was Viv Richards against England. He scored 100 off 56 balls."

"Absolutely correct," Jo said admiringly. There was a big groan from the Glory Gardens supporters and then the Aussies all rushed forward to congratulate their team. Jo was the first to shake hands with Sepo, who had been the undoubted star of the evening. It may have only been a quiz but I was getting tired of always coming second to Woolagong.

HOME TEAM	GLORY GARDENS V WOOLAGONG	AWAY TEAM	AT WHITMART PRIORY. DATE AUG.4TH..

INNINGS OF WOOLAGONG............ **TOSS WON BY** W'GONG **WEATHER** SUNNY.

	BATSMAN	RUNS SCORED	HOW OUT	BOWLER	SCORE
1	D.HOLDRIGHT	4·4·1·3·2·2·1·2·2	bowled	LEAR	21
2	I.SUSZ	4·1·2·1·2·2·4·1·1·1·1·1	NOT	OUT	22
3	R.GONZALES	2·2·2·2·4·1·1·1·2·1·1·2·4·1	NOT	OUT	26
4					
5					
6					
7					
8					
9					
10					
11					

FALL OF WICKETS

	1	2	3	4	5	6	7	8	9	10
SCORE	47									
BAT NO	1									

BYES	1·1·1·2·1·1·1
LBYES	2·1·1
WIDES	1·1·1·2·1
NO BALLS	

TOTAL EXTRAS	19
TOTAL FOR WKTS	88 1

SCORE AT A GLANCE

BOWLING ANALYSIS ⊙ NO BALL + WIDE

	BOWLER	1	2	3	4	5	6	7	8	9	10	11	12	13	OVS	MDS	RUNS	WKT
1	M.LEAR	4	4 2 2	X	2 2 2 4	X									6	0	25	1
2	J.GUNN	1 1 1 4	3 2 2 3 2	X											3	0	21	0
3	H.KNIGHT	1	2 4	X											3	0	8	0
4	C.SEBASIEN	1	1	M	X										5	1	6	0
5	E.DAVIES	1	M	2	1	1	M	M	X						9	3	7	0
6	T.VELLACOTT	1	4	M	1	X									5	1	8	0
7																		
8																		
9																		

Chapter Thirteen

The next morning was sunny again and it was already getting very hot by the time we were ready to start at half past eleven.

"The weather's not going to save us," said Cal.

"No," I said. "It's win or lose – it won't be a draw."

"Cheer up. A couple of quick wickets and we're back in it," Cal said, ever the optimist.

"And who's going to take them?"

"If you're asking, I'd start with Marty at the top and maybe Tylan up the hill." It wasn't a bad idea. I certainly didn't want to risk Jacky at the Herr Dryer end.

Jacky arrived looking ready for war. I wasted no time in telling him what Kiddo had said about the chucker but he just laughed at any suggestion that the Aussie umpire might not be biased in favour of his own team. He wasn't pleased to be told that I wasn't going to bowl him at the start.

Marty worked up a head of steam from the top end. He found the edge again and again and it wasn't his fault that the ball kept flying into spaces or through Frankie's gloves or straight past Ohbert at third-man. Ohbert was still limping from his blow on the toe and was even slower than usual out on the boundary. Frankie, too, was a bit green-looking – almost certainly because of his gluttony the previous evening, though his theory was that the Aussies had poisoned his food.

He was too sick even to make a sarcastic comment when,

astonishingly, Jo missed the umpire's signal for a leg-bye because she was so deep in conversation with Sepo. Tylan took time to find his line and length and Robbie Gonzales was quick to punish anything loose. The score rocketed up to 100 and before we knew it Woolagong had passed our total of 123 for the loss of just the single wicket.

Then, out of nowhere, Marty produced the sort of ball which makes him such a feared bowler. It swung into the opening batsman and cut away off the bounce. He had to play at it and it flew off the edge. Frankie did well to follow it and, at last, he took a clean catch. A weak smile spread across his face but soon disappeared when Marty gave him a hearty slap on the back and he nearly threw up. Stacks Stachiewitz got a brute of a yorker first ball and survived a huge appeal for lbw.

Then it was Tylan's turn. Three times in a row he spun the ball past the right-hander's bat and then he picked up the big prize of Robbie Gonzales, who top edged a sweep straight into the hands of Erica at square-leg.

With two new batters at the wicket, I was able to go a little more on to the attack. George Kynaston left with a golden duck after another Marty yorker flattened his middle stump and, suddenly, at 130 for four there was just a glimmer of hope that we could bowl them out with only a modest first innings lead.

Both Mart and Tylan continued to beat the bat, but they were tiring and it was time for the first bowling change of the morning. Erica and I bowled in tandem for ten overs without giving much away but we failed to get the vital breakthrough. Just before lunch, I gave the ball to Cal. He struck with his first ball. The batter played all round a straight one and it clipped the off bail. Then, in the final over before the break, there was a terrible mix up between the two batsmen. "Yes ... no ... no ... yes, er, NO ... GET BACK!" went Cameron Armstrong and they both finished up at the same end. Erica picked up, ran in with the ball and took off the bails. Stacks was the one who had to go – he'd made 24.

The score at lunch was 178 for six; a lead of 55.

"So why didn't I get a bowl all morning?" Jacky demanded when we were back in the dressing room.

"It didn't work out that way. I guess you'll be on after lunch," I said evasively.

"We've given them 99 runs this morning – and you turn your back on one of your two main strike bowlers. I call that madness."

"Call it what you like, but fortunately I still make the decisions round here, not you," I said crossly.

Jacky looked as though he could kill me but he turned and walked away without another word. After lunch he'd calmed down a bit and he tried again. "Sorry, Hook," he said. "All I want is a chance to get at those arrogant Australians."

"You will. But I'd rather you were thinking about getting wickets, instead of getting personal," I said.

"Just watch me," said Jacky.

After the break Cal completed his interrupted over and I finally threw the ball to Jacky. At first it didn't look as if it was a wise decision. Some controlled slogging by Armstrong and Slim Squirrell brought up the 200 in no time. Jacky was pitching a fraction short and I told him so. He was a lot calmer than he'd been before lunch and the gamble of bowling him from the Herr Dryer end hadn't yet resulted in all-out warfare – even when the umpire turned down an optimistic shout for lbw. But I knew the powder keg could go up at any moment.

With the score on 207, Jacky ran in to start his third over. Cameron Armstrong stepped down the track to him and flat-batted a good length ball for four through mid-off. Jacky looked at him coldly. "I bet you can't do that again," he said.

"Watch me, mate," said Cameron.

Jacky walked back slowly. I wondered whether he'd have the sense to try his slower ball. He ran in faster than usual and bowled. The line was just outside off-stump and yes – he'd held the ball back. I spotted it, but Cameron didn't – he played his drive too early and got a snick. Frankie hurled himself forward on to his stomach to get a glove under the ball and beamed with pleasure as he rolled on his back and held the prize aloft.

"Howzaaaat," Jacky screamed at Herr Dryer. For a moment there was no reaction and then the umpire looked over to Sid Burns at square-leg.

"Of course it carried," Jacky began to protest. Sid Burns nodded to confirm the catch was good.

"Then it's out," said Herr Dryer, raising his finger.

Jacky looked at me and his mouth dropped open in utter disbelief.

"Outrageous. Is that a pig I see flying over the pavilion?" said Tylan.

Frankie ran half the length of the pitch to congratulate Jacky as if he was a long-lost friend. All the bad feeling between them had been completely forgotten.

The next player on strike was Si Bannerjee. He went back to a fast delivery from Jacky and the ball hammered into his back pad.

"Out!" said Herr Dryer, almost before Jacky could appeal.

"What did he have for lunch?" asked Tylan, incredulously.

"We'd better find out and serve it up for the rest of the weekend," said Frankie, who was looking a lot better since the break – somehow he'd managed two helpings of pudding. The whole team was still celebrating the miracle of two Herr Dryer decisions going our way when Dean Caroota arrived to take strike.

"You'll never get a better chance for a hat trick, Jack," shouted Frankie. Dean scowled but said nothing.

"Yorker," Jacky whispered to me. I brought the whole field in to close catching positions and we waited. Jacky turned at the end of his run and gave Deano a long stare. He pounded in, down came the front foot hard and everything went into the delivery. It was right in the block hole. Caroota hopped in the air and tried to get his bat down at the last moment.

The ball grazed the outside of his boot and ripped into the stumps. There was a huge cheer from the players which echoed round the ground. The spectators jumped to their feet to applaud the hat trick. Dean looked wearily at his stumps for a moment and slouched off.

"Pity you missed his toe," Frankie said uncharitably. Jacky was hopping up and down, grinning from ear to ear. It was his first hat trick and he kept punching the air with delight and shouting "Out!" until Dean had disappeared into the pavilion.

Jacky's fourth wicket came in his next over. Jack Grylls missed five balls in a row which all flashed past his off-stump; the sixth was on target and he missed again. With his late burst Jacky had taken four for four in two overs and terminated the Woolagong innings. He couldn't resist a taunt of "I told you so" at me as we walked off – but I didn't care a bit.

Woolagong finished on 215 – a lead of 92. It was a huge deficit to make up, but it could have been a lot worse.

There was a ten-minute break between innings and then a tricky forty minutes for us to negotiate before tea. Kiddo and Wally came into our dressing room. Kiddo was looking a little more cheerful and he said we should play our normal game and not go completely on the defensive. Wally told us we'd done excellently to keep their lead to under a hundred.

"It would have been a lot less if it hadn't been for their top scorer," said Cal.

"You mean Robbie Gonzales?" asked Wally.

"No. Extras. He got 44, and 21 were byes." Cal said, with a nod in Frankie's direction.

Frankie grabbed the scorebook. "Remind me, Cal. Who was it who took those two brilliant catches? Oh look, it says here 'F. Allen'."

Cal and Matthew took to the field with all the hopes of the team resting on their shoulders. It wasn't hard to imagine how fired up Dean Caroota and Jack Grylls would be at the start of the innings. Matthew, as usual, took first strike and survived a fiery salvo from Caroota bowling from the top end. Both the bowlers showed good control, holding a perfect line on or just outside off-stump, and Jack Grylls gave Cal a couple of nasty frights as he dipped the ball into him at pace. After nine overs we began to think they'd survived the worst, particularly when Dean Caroota was rested. But then Jack Grylls got one to stop on Matthew and he pushed back a simple return catch to the bowler. We were 15 for one.

Then came the nightmare. Azzie edged his first ball straight into slip's hands and although he fumbled, he managed to knock it up in the air and Slim Squirrell latched on to the rebound. Erica came in on the hat trick ball and survived a confident lbw appeal. After a wonderful in-form start to the season, Erica's recent run of scores have been miserable, mainly thanks to Herr Dryer and his terrible umpiring decisions. She looked confident today, though, and played Si Bannerjee with great skill, until he lured her forward to play a flighted leg break and went past the outside of the bat. Slim flicked the off bail in the air and roared his appeal at the square-leg umpire. Erica stood her ground. As far as we could see, she hadn't moved her back foot and it was firmly rooted just behind the line. "Out," said Herr Dryer. "You lifted your foot."

"But I didn't," protested Erica.

"You're out, young lady," the umpire said firmly.

Erica took a deep breath and walked, without another trace of protest – at least until she was back in the pavilion. I heard the crash of her bat flying across the changing room when I was halfway to the crease.

I only had to face one ball before tea and then watch Cal survive a maiden over at the other end.

"Was she out?" Cal asked me when we were walking off together.

"She didn't think so."

119

"What we need is a third umpire. It's a pity the TV news camera doesn't do action replays."

"It'll take more than a third umpire to save us now," I said, looking up at the scoreboard. It read 23 for two – but it should have been three. Jo and Sepo had forgotten to put up the last wicket because they were so busy talking. "We need at least two players to score fifties and, with the batting we've got to come, it had better be you and me."

After tea Si and George Kynaston were almost impossible to get away. Si came round the wicket, bowling into the rough made by the seamers' follow-through. He was turning it sharply across me and getting one or two to bounce awkwardly, too.

Robbie brought in the field to stop the singles and encourage us to hit over the top. Both of us resisted the temptation, so ten overs were bowled for just seven runs. Then Cal ran himself out. Whether he was frustrated by the slow scoring or had just lost his concentration, I don't know – but he set off for a second run with Caroota at third-man already holding the ball in his hand. The throw to the keeper was fast and low and on target and Cal didn't have a prayer.

Mack made his way to the wicket with more confidence and determination than he'd shown for over a week. "It's time for someone to boss the bowling," he said. "If we carry on like this they'll strangle the life out of us."

"You know what Kiddo said. Play your game. I'm going to hang in at one end and hope I'm still there tomorrow morning."

"And I'm going to show Woolagong what Western Australians are made of," Mack said, sounding more like his old self every moment.

After taking a look at Si Bannerjee for the best part of an over, Mack chanced his arm and went down the wicket to him. The hit was good and clean and crossed the ropes on the second bounce. It was the first boundary of the innings.

Immediately Robbie brought Dean Caroota back. Mack

didn't flinch. He middled the first ball, blocked out a lightning-fast yorker and then thick edged down to third-man for two. Deano didn't like that. He stood in the middle of the pitch and made Mack run round him for the second run.

"G'day, sport," said Mack. "You directing the traffic?"

"Next ball you're dead," Caroota hissed angrily, pointing a finger at Mack.

Deano put an extra kilo of effort into his next delivery. It was a truly venomous ball, fired just short of a length into Mack's ribs. He went to pull, but the ball was on him fast and hit his bottom hand as the bat came through. Psycho Caroota sneered and I knew immediately that Mack was in trouble. The ball dropped down in front of him and he tore off his glove. His middle finger was bleeding round the nail and turning purple.

"Get off and get that seen to, lad," said Sid Burns. Mack flexed his fingers and tried to pick up his bat but finally he agreed to take a breather. Several of the Woolagong team had gathered round to help but Dean Caroota kept well away. He walked slowly back to the start of his run, ready for the next batsman. He certainly wasn't going to waste his breath on showing sympathy for Mack. Mack stared at him as he left, as if to say, I'll be back and I'll remember that.

Frankie was typically brim-full of confidence. "Here I am, Hook. Your worries are over. You just carry on doing your Matthew impersonation and I'll smack it about."

He allowed himself one ball from Dean Caroota to get his eye in and then pulled the second fiercely over square-leg for four. "Just keep serving them up, Deano," he said with a smile when the big fast bowler came down the track to give him an eyeball-to-eyeball glare.

An even bigger hit from a George Kynaston half-volley cleared the ropes at long-on by some distance. It was a fearsome shot, like a forearm jab delivered with tremendous power, and the crowd let Frankie know how much they enjoyed the big six. The OBA even allowed themselves a rare chant of "Frankie! Frankie!" before returning to sing the praises of their real hero again.

I faced a whole over of Dean Caroota on overdrive and I managed to keep him out and even glanced him for a couple of runs on the leg side. Frankie's taunt that I was "doing a Matthew" didn't bother me at all. I just hoped he wouldn't get too crazy and throw his wicket away. But I didn't say anything.

In the next over he played an even more astonishing shot – a flat-bat drive on the off side which went in the air straight over extra cover for four. Frankie was getting more and more excited. He took an enormous heave at the next ball and it flew high in the air off a thick outside edge. Deep mid-off waited and waited for it to come to earth. Drop it, I prayed. But he stood his ground and took a clean catch. We were 56 for five – probably six, if Mack couldn't bat again. It was beginning to look hopeless.

Tylan made his way uncertainly to the wicket and I kept him away from the strike for the best part of the next half-hour. It was just as well because, when he was forced to face the bowling, he showed no signs of getting his bat anywhere near the ball apart from once, an edge to the keeper and Slim fortunately put him down.

The return of Jack Grylls finally accounted for Tylan. He was clean bowled for one of the longest ducks on record. I watched to see if Mack would return, but no, it was Jacky who made his way to the wicket. We had struggled to 65 for six, still 27 runs short of making Woolagong bat again and, as far as I knew, with only Marty and Ohbert to come. It looked desperate. I had scored just 15 runs in the 25 overs that I'd spent out in the middle. It was easily my slowest innings on record, and I began to wonder if I'd got the tactics all wrong. Should I have tried to hit us out of trouble? Was it time now to chance my arm, with only the tail enders to come?

Jacky had a message from Kiddo. "He says, whatever you do, be there at the end of play."

"Fair enough," I said. "I don't fancy being knocked over in two days either."

"I'm with you," said Jacky. "Glory Gardens doesn't give up that easily against a bunch of cheating Aussies."

Cameron Armstrong came on at the bottom end and I played out yet another maiden. A big yawn from Slim Squirrell said exactly what he thought of me. "I'm going to put myself to sleep tonight thinking of your innings, Hooker." I didn't reply but I woke him up next over when I got an inside edge to a jack-knifing in-cutter from Grylls. The ball bounced on to my chest and through to the keeper. It was dropping on Slim all the time and he threw himself forward but I thought he took the ball on the half-volley. Nevertheless, Jack Grylls appealed and Herr Dryer raised his finger. I bowed my head and turned for the long walk back.

"Not out," shouted a voice behind me. It was Robbie Gonzales. "It didn't carry – I saw it all the way."

I looked at Herr Dryer and then at Sid Burns at square-leg for a decision. Sid shrugged his shoulders. "I didn't get a clear view. But if the skipper says not out, I'll take his word for it."

"I had my eyes closed," said Slim. "It might have been on the bounce."

"Not out," Robbie said firmly again.

"Fair enough," Dryer said expressionlessly.

I mumbled a word of thanks and returned to face Jack Grylls. Somehow Jacky and I managed to struggle to 73 by close of play, without losing another wicket. "We live to fight another day," he said as we walked off. I'd scored just 20 breathtakingly boring runs in over two hours' play.

HOME TEAM GLORY GARDENS V WOOLAGONG		AWAY TEAM	AT WHITMARSH PRIORY DATE AUG 4TH-5TH	
INNINGS OF WOOLAGONG		TOSS WON BY WOLGONG	WEATHER SUNNY	

BATSMAN	RUNS SCORED	HOW OUT	BOWLER	SCORE
1 D.HOLDRIGHT	4·4·1·3·2·2·1·2·2	bowled	LEAR	21
2 I.SUSZ	4·1·2·1·2·2·4·1·1·1·1·1·4·1·4·2·1	ct ALLEN	LEAR	34
3 R.GONZALES	2·2·2·2·4·1·1·1·2·1·1·2·4·1·2·2·2·4·1·2·1·1·1	ct DAVIES	VELLACOTT	42
4 T.STACHIEWITZ	2·1·2·2·1·1·2·1·4·1·1·1·2·2·1	Run	OUT	24
5 G.KYNASTON		bowled	LEAR	0
6 L.H-KIRBY	2·1·4·1·4·2·1·1·3	bowled	SEBASTIEN	20
7 C.ARMSTRONG	4·1·1·2·1·4·2·4	ct ALLEN	GUNN	19
8 M.SQUIRRELL	1·4·1·1·4	NOT	OUT	11
9 S.BANNERJEE		lbw	GUNN	0
10 D.CARDOTA		bowled	GUNN	0
11 J.GRYLLS		bowled	GUNN	0

FALL OF WICKETS											BYES	1·1·2·1·1·1·1·2·1·1 2·1·1·2·2	21	TOTAL EXTRAS	44
SCORE	47	125	129	130	17	178	207	20	207	215	L.BYES	2·1·2·1·1·1·2	12	TOTAL FOR	215
BAT NO	1	2	3	5	6	4	7	9	10	11	WIDES	1·1·2·1·4	10	ALL	
											NO BALLS	1	1	WKTS	OUT

SCORE AT A GLANCE

BOWLER	BOWLING ANALYSIS ⊙ NO BALL + WIDE													OVS	MDS	RUNS	WKT
	1	2	3	4	5	6	7	8	9	10	11	12	13				
1 M.LEAR														13	0	47	3
2																	
3 J.GUNN														7	1	37	4
4 H.KNIGHT														7	1	18	0
5 C.SEBASTIEN														10	1	25	1
6 E.DAVIES														14	5	13	0
7																	
8 T.VELLACOTT														13	1	42	1
9																	

HOME TEAM	GLORY GARDENS V WOOLAGONG	AWAY TEAM	AT WHITMART PRIORY DATE Aug 5th

INNINGS OF GLORY GARDENS   TOSS WON BY W'gong   WEATHER Sunny

BATSMAN	RUNS SCORED	HOW OUT	BOWLER	SCORE
1 M. ROSE	1·1·1·2·1	c & b	GRYLLS	6
2 C. SEBASTIEN	2·1·2·1·1·1	RUN	OUT	8
3 A. NAZAR		ct SQUIRRELL	GRYLLS	0
4 E. DAVIES	2·2	st SQUIRRELL	BANNERJEE	4
5 H. KNIGHT	1·1·1·2·1·2·1·2·1·1·1·1·2·2	NOT	OUT	20
6 T. McCURDY	4·2	RETIRED	HURT	6
7 F. ALLEN	4·6·4	ct SUS Z	KYNASTON	14
8 T. VELLACOTT		bowled	GRYLLS	0
9 J. GUNN	1	NOT	OUT	1
10				
11				

FALL OF WICKETS

	BYES	1·2·1·2		6	TOTAL EXTRAS	14

SCORE	15	15	22	31	56	65	7	8	9	10	L.BYES	1·1·1·1·1		6	TOTAL FOR	73
BAT NO	1	3	4	2	7	8					WIDES			(	WKTS	6
											NO BALLS	1		1		

SCORE AT A GLANCE

BOWLER	BOWLING ANALYSIS ⊙ NO BALL + WIDE													OVS	MDS	RUNS	WKT
	1	2	3	4	5	6	7	8	9	10	11	12	13				
1 D. CARDOTA	M	:	:	:	2	:	X	:	2	:	M	M	X	10	3	14	0
2 J. GRYLLS	:	:	+	:	M	W	:	M	X	:	W	M	:	X	11	4	12	3
3 S. BANNERJEE	:	:	W	M	M	:	M	:	:	:	4	X		9	3	11	1
4 G. KYNASTON	:	:	M	:	:	:	:	2	W	2	:		10	1	21	1
5 C. ARMSTRONG	M	:	:	:	X									3	1	3	0
6																	
7																	
8																	
9																	

Chapter Fourteen

Much to my surprise I slept well, though I had a strange dream about being chased round the boundary by Ohbert's Barmy Army and jumping in the canal to escape.

Next morning the not-out batters; Jacky, Mack and Marty, were all at the ground early for net practice. Mack's finger was a nasty colour and very swollen, but he insisted that he could hold a bat. Ohbert arrived early, too, and he even put on his pads and had a net, though the sight of him missing every ball bowled at him didn't necessarily raise the team's morale.

"We need to set ourselves small targets," said Mack. "First we score 19 runs to make them bat again. Then we build a lead. Ten at a time."

"Make it five," I said. "But you're right – little by little, that's the only way."

"It's pretty hopeless," said Marty. "Even if we get a lead of 50, they'll knock them off in no time."

"Never," Mack said defiantly. "Think positive. We've got four wickets left. Let 'em see that Glory Gardens doesn't go down without a big fight."

I told Mack to come in after the next wicket fell. The four of us agreed a plan and I remember thinking that, if it came off, it would be one of the greatest miracles in cricket history, but it was better than going out there and getting walked all over. Of course, the plan didn't include Ohbert – we all knew he'd make it up as he went along.

The pitch looked even better than the previous day. Jacky and I walked out to the middle in silence. There was nothing to say. We knew the score, the first thing to do was to avoid the humiliation of an innings' defeat.

I was on strike and it was no surprise to discover that I would be facing Dean Caroota and an ultra-attacking field. Woolagong were bristling with confidence. As far as they were concerned it was game over before lunch. All they had to do was polish off the tail. I defended the first two balls, let the third go by outside the off-stump, and then clumped the next one in the air over mid-wicket for four. Deano's fifth ball was pitched very short and called a wide by Herr Dryer; the one after was over-pitched and I drove it hard through the covers for another boundary. I could feel the players and the spectators suddenly sit up and take an interest in the proceedings.

Jacky managed to fend off Jack Grylls's first over with a straight bat and we got the bonus of a couple of leg-byes. I faced Caroota again. The first task was to knock him out of the attack. Robbie set a slightly more defensive field to me although he kept in a slip and a silly mid-off. Dean dropped his pace slightly, trying to tempt me outside the off-stump. I resisted twice, waiting for the half-volley. And when it came I carved it through the covers for my third boundary of the morning. Another single came off the last ball off the over and I realised I was beginning to enjoy myself.

Jack Grylls, bowling a nagging length, offered little to drive, but I worked him off my hip twice – for a two and a single – to bring the scores level. There was a huge cheer from the pavilion, led by Frankie, and an even louder one from the OBA, although they probably didn't know what they were cheering. Then it was Woolagong's turn to celebrate. Jacky got a nasty in-cutter which just clipped his off bail. He'd scored only one run, but our partnership of 27 was the highest of the innings so far.

Now the strategy changed. We had decided that Mack should play his natural attacking game and that I wouldn't try and protect him from the bowling. It was a high-risk plan for both of us to go on the attack, and it nearly came unstuck with the first ball he received. He got an outside edge to Dean Caroota and it flew at catchable height between the keeper and slip, but they got in each other's way and down it went. Mack got off the mark with a straight drive past the bowler for two.

We continued to attack the bowling of Caroota and work Jack Grylls for singles where we could, and it was from a leg glance for two that I brought up the hundred. Pandemonium broke out round the ground. There were whistles and horns and chants. It was hard to believe, amidst all the jubilation that, in real terms, we were 8 for seven and staring defeat in the face. But the Glory Gardens' supporters hadn't had a lot to shout about on the first two days, so who could blame them.

I took six from Dean Caroota's next over, including a lovely late cut which sped away down the hill to the boundary. Looking up at the scoreboard I realised that I was on 47. I could scarcely believe it. After scoring 20 in two hours, I'd added 27 from fewer than nine overs this morning. The score was 106 for seven. Robbie looked a little shaken by the events so far. Things hadn't quite gone to plan. He took off Dean Caroota, after only four overs. Round one to us.

Round two came with my 50 from a neat glide down to third-man. To my surprise the bowler, Jack Grylls, and Robbie all joined in the applause. "Good knock, mate," said Jack, giving me a tap on the back as I passed him.

I raised my bat to the pavilion and Frankie shouted, "Now for the ton, Hooker."

As expected, Robbie replaced Deano with Si Bannerjee, who immediately turned three balls past Mack's outside edge. The fourth delivery was a googly. I don't think Mack picked it, although he might have been expecting one and chanced his arm. He swung with the spin, caught the ball dead in the meat of his bat and it took off like a guided missile, easily clearing the short boundary opposite the pavilion. "Six to England! We want Ohbert!" cried the OBA.

As the field went back, we started to push the ones and twos as planned. I timed the sweep against a Si Bannerjee googly so sweetly that it went for four and then I dropped my bat on the top-spinner and ran a cheeky single to bring up 130. I suddenly realised that the last two partnerships had doubled our score. Perhaps nothing was impossible after all.

Now Mack was having fun too. He slogged another four against the spinner and we met in the middle. "Not going too badly, mate?" he said with a broad grin. "They've all gone a bit quiet, haven't they?"

It was true. Woolagong were getting worried and the sledging had almost completely dried up.

Jack Grylls's spell came to an end. He had bowled seven overs this morning and taken one for 20. But his statistics for the innings were: 18 overs; 4 maidens; 32 runs; 4 wickets.

The partnership with Mack came to an end in Si's next over. Mack holed out on the mid-wicket boundary, going for another big slog over the top. I couldn't complain. He'd died fighting and clubbed a valiant 29; together we'd put on 48 runs.

Marty had elected to go for his shots too. He hoiked the spinner over cover-point from his very first ball and we ran three. I wondered, for a moment, whether I should try and calm him down, but there wasn't much point. If Marty and I were going to set them even a modest target, he might as well chance his arm. A powerful cross-bat smash dispatched Cameron Armstrong to the long-off boundary and Marty's version of a cover drive brought two more off the edge.

With only Ohbert to come, I knew I had to make the most of what time I had left in the middle. I reverse swept Si Bannerjee and was lucky to direct a top edge over the top of fly slip. That brought up the 150. Another mis-hit lobbed back over the bowler's outstretched hand went for two more.

With the score on 157 Marty lost his leg stump to a good in-swinger. I quickly calculated our lead . . . 65. If only we could push it over the hundred. If only Ohbert wasn't coming in next. If only . . .

After a long delay, when I began to wonder whether he'd forgotten all about batting and gone home, Ohbert limped on to the pitch. Even the pensioners joined in with the OBA to give him a rousing welcome. So far this morning we'd followed a plan and it had gone amazingly well but, with Ohbert's arrival, all plans were abandoned. It was everyone for himself.

Ohbert survived four balls of Cameron Armstrong's over which included a delivery that rapped him on the pads and would have been a straightforward lbw if it hadn't first been called a no-ball. He could also have been run out twice and caught off the other three balls, but the close fielders fumbled and Ohbert lived on.

I decided to attack the leg-spinner while there was still time. Down the wicket I went to the first ball of Si's next over and planted it back over the bowler's head – but long-on ran round and kept us to a single. Ohbert wasn't wearing quite as much padding as in the first innings but the bruised toe was an extra handicap. He wasn't so much running as hopping between the wickets. Ohbert played two bizarre forward defensive shots completely down the wrong line and then opted for an exotic reverse sweep to Si's top-spinner. The ball took the faintest inside edge, bounced on to his bad toe and ricocheted off Slim Squirrell's glove. We ran two, although I nearly lapped Ohbert who was moving like a one-legged chicken. The next ball hit Ohbert's pad outside the off-stump and, as the Aussies appealed in vain, he hopped down the track again for a single. If Slim had thrown to the bowler's end, instead of shying at the stumps, Ohbert would have been run out by a mile.

Expecting the curtains to come down at any moment

I aimed a slog sweep against the spin at the next leg break and I was as astonished as delighted that it shot through the leg-side field for four.

"166 for nine," I said out loud, as I looked up at the scoreboard. I vaguely remember noticing that I had 70 of them. Could we squeeze another five or ten, or even 15? Even 15 more would give us a lead of only 88, but at least it would be something to bowl at.

Ohbert surprised everyone, himself included probably, by going down the wicket to every ball of Armstrong's next over and padding him away. Although there were a couple of appeals for lbw, he was so far down the track on both occasions that even Herr Dryer couldn't bring himself to give him out.

Dean Caroota came back and, unfortunately, his first ball to me went for a bye. Although it didn't seem quite so unfortunate when Ohbert hooked him for four. It wasn't really a hook, of course, but the ball was short and Ohbert ducked and stuck his bat up in the air at the same time. The ball glanced off it and ran all the way to the fine-leg boundary. Dean generously followed that with two wides and then three balls which bounced just over Ohbert's middle stump – Ohbert turned them all into yorkers by hopping down the wicket to them. Seven off the over; we'd now stretched the lead to 81.

I cracked the first ball of Armstrong's next over past extra cover for two and followed that with a neat leg glance for a single. By now I'd decided not to waste energy trying to protect Ohbert from the strike – after all Ohbert could do anything. As if to prove it he nearly knocked Slim Squirrell's head off his shoulders with a wild swing of the bat and the keeper gave away two more byes. Next Ohbert set off on a suicide run after a short ball bounced off glove and pad straight back to the bowler. Luckily I was backing up a long way and panicked Armstrong into a direct shy, which narrowly missed the stumps.

His next ball was slightly over-pitched and I opened my shoulders and on-drove hard to the long-on boundary. The deep fielder ran round and dived spectacularly, but he managed only to deflect it into the rope before clattering into a deckchair and dumping an elderly spectator in a heap on the ground.

The on-drive is one of the hardest shots in the game because you pick up the ball in front of your left leg, and it's very easy to overbalance as you play the drive. The secret is to get well over the ball and keep your head as still as possible.

Lunch was one ball away, although I didn't know it. My heart was thumping, my mouth was dry and I didn't even consider defending against the next delivery from Armstrong. It was just short of a length and outside the off-stump and I went down on one knee and drove hard on the up. The ball took a thick inside edge and smashed into the stumps. We were all out for 183. We'd scored exactly 110 runs in the morning's session for the last four wickets. Not bad, I thought, as I walked back with Ohbert hobbling alongside me. Not bad but not enough.

HOME TEAM	GLORY GARDENS V WOOLAGONG	AWAY TEAM	AT WHITMART PRIORY DATE AUG 5TH-6TH

INNINGS OF GLORY GARDENS **TOSS WON BY** W'GONG **WEATHER** HOT

BATSMAN	RUNS SCORED	HOW OUT	BOWLER	SCORE
1 M. ROSE	1.1.1.2.1	c×b	GRYLLS	6
2 C. SEBASTIEN	2.1.2.1.1.1	RUN	OUT	8
3 A. NAZAR		c SQUIRRELL	GRYLLS	0
4 E. DAVIES	2.2	st SQUIRRELL	BANNERJEE	4
5 H. KNIGHT	1.1.1.1.2.1.2.1.2.1.1.1.2.2.4.4.4.1.2.1.1.2 2.2.4.2(49).1.1.1.4.1.2.1.2.2.1.4.2.1.4	bowled	ARMSTRONG	77
6 T. McCURDY	4.2.2.1.1.6.1.1.2.1.4.1.2	c KIRBY	BANNERJEE	29
7 F. ALLEN	4.6.4	c SUSZ	KYNASTON	14
8 T. VELLACOTT		bowled	GRYLLS	0
9 J. GUNN	1	bowled	GRYLLS	1
10 M. LEAR	3.4.2	bowled	ARMSTRONG	9
11 P. BENNETT	2.4.1	NOT	OUT	7

FALL OF WICKETS

SCORE	15	15	22	31	56	65	92	140	157	183
	1	2	3	4	5	6	7	8	9	10
BAT NO	1	3	4	2	7	8	9	6	10	5

BYES	1.2.1.2.1.1.1.2	11	TOTAL EXTRAS	28
LBYES	1.1.1.1.1.2.1.1.1	11	TOTAL	183
WIDES	1.1.1	4	FOR	ALL
NO BALLS	1.1	2	WKTS	OUT

SCORE AT A GLANCE

BOWLER	BOWLING ANALYSIS ⊙ NO BALL + WIDE													OVS	MDS	RUNS	WKT
	1	2	3	4	5	6	7	8	9	10	11	12	13				
1 D. CARDOTA	M			2			2.4	2		M	M	✕	4				
2			2	4	4									15	3	43	0
3 J. GRYLLS	2	1	⊙	M	W	2	M	✕	1	1	M	2	✕				
4	M	2	2	1		2		2						18	4	32	4
5 S. BANNERJEE	2	2	M	M	1	M	1		✕	6	1	41					
6	4	2	2	2	4	✕								16	3	47	2
7 G. KYNASTON	1	M				2		W 6.4	2	1	✕			10	1	21	1
8 C. ARMSTRONG	M	2			✕	2	M	4 W						7	2	18	2
9																	

Chapter Fifteen

The mood at lunch was one of grim determination. Everyone knew the score now – if we didn't take ten Woolagong wickets before they reached 92, we'd lost the test match. Even Frankie was relatively quiet, and he didn't eat quite as much as usual either.

When we returned to our changing room Mack found another anonymous message, like the first, lying on top of his kitbag. He showed it to Cal, Frankie and me later – we were still the only ones to know about Ned Kelly. It was a very strange message indeed:

> *Sorry about what we wrote. That was a brilliant knock!*
> *Good luck this afternoon.*
> Ned Kelly

It was in the same handwriting as the first note.

"Seems you've gone from traitor to hero, Mack," Cal said, looking as puzzled as the rest of us.

"It doesn't make any sense," I said.

"Perhaps it's a plan to confuse me before we go out to field," suggested Mack.

"Any idea who Ned Kelly is?" Frankie asked Mack.

"No. It could be anyone. Dean Caroota. Sepo. Herr Dryer, even."

"And then it might not be a Woolagonger at all," said Frankie.

"That's crazy. Who else would . . ."

"Someone who didn't want you to play. Perhaps they just wanted you to think they were Australian."

"And who would pull a stunt like that?"

"I'm not sure," said Frankie. "But I think I know how to find out."

I left them still discussing the letter, partly because I thought Frankie was talking rubbish as usual, but also I wanted to have a word with Marty and Jacky before the afternoon session began. Woolagong needed just 92 runs to win the game and, on this pitch, that should be a pushover. Our only chance was to take early wickets and put the pressure back on them. That was down to our opening bowlers. We agreed Marty would bowl flat out to an attacking field while Jacky, from the bottom end, concentrated on an off-stump line, just short of a length.

Kiddo came over and wished us good luck. I asked him if he'd got any instructions or useful ideas. He shook his head. "You're in charge, kiddo. You know your team. Win or lose, I know they'll do their best."

We took the field to a fanfare of trumpets from the jazz band and I talked to both Frankie and Mack about keeping the fielders on their toes. The keeper has a big role to play as motivator and Mack, our best fielder by far, leads by example. But I needn't have worried; everyone was keyed up and ready to go. I set an attacking field, with only Jacky and Ohbert outside the ring, and Marty took a deep breath, ran in and bowled. The ball came off the track at pace and the batsman left it. It was a risky choice because it missed the off-stump by a coat of varnish and hammered into Frankie's gloves. The crowd went "Ooooooh".

"A millimetre to the right next ball and you've got him, Mart," cried Frankie. You could feel the tension round the ground. The spectators picked up on Marty's determination and they were willing him on. The next four balls were fast and right on the spot. But then he strayed on to leg stump and Dai Holdright worked him away for a couple of runs. I've hardly ever seen Mart so angry with himself – he knew he'd released the pressure by giving away easy runs.

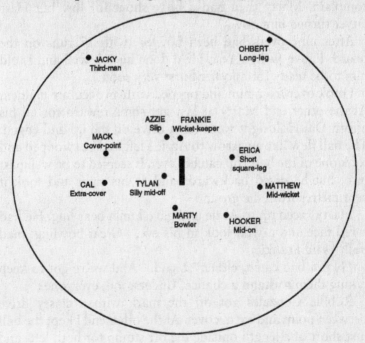

Jacky's first over was straight and he nearly got through Ivan Susz's defence with his quicker ball. Woolagong were biding their time, however. Their strategy seemed to be to blunt our attack bowlers and then pick off the runs at leisure – they had two whole sessions to score 92 runs, so why hurry?

Marty, roaring downhill, was bowling faster and faster. A thick inside edge flew desperately close to the stumps and beat the diving Frankie. Ohbert stumbled after it on the long-leg boundary. To be fair he did his best to stop the ball, but he put his bad foot in a rabbit hole just as he reached it and dived over the top.

Marty groaned and asked me to put a real fielder down there, but I didn't want Ohbert in a close catching position either, so he stayed at long-leg for both bowlers. It was a long, slow walk for him at the end of each over, and he held up the play every time, but I couldn't help that and Ohbert didn't complain. Marty then had a huge shout for lbw but Herr Dryer turned him down.

After nine overs had been bowled, with 17 runs on the board, I gave Jacky a rest. He'd done his job well and I told him to be ready for another burst very soon.

I took over from him and opened with an accurate maiden. At the other end Marty at last got some reward for all his effort. Dai Holdright went for a drive on the up and edged. The ball flew like an arrow to Azzie's left and he swooped and took one of the best slip catches ever. It seemed to be well past him, but he dived backwards and to his right and took it centimetres from the ground.

Marty raced up to Azzie and gave him a bear hug. He had a red face and a wild look in his eye. "Great bowling, mad bull," said Frankie.

"Not a bad catch, either," I said. "And we've got to keep taking them to stand a chance. Understood, everyone?"

Robbie Gonzales got off the mark with a classy drive between point and extra cover. At the other end I kept the ball just short of a length outside the off-stump for both left- and right-hander. The opener drove me for two and then Robbie played a glide down to third-man for a single.

I gave Frankie the signal to come up to the stumps and bowled my slower ball. It was straight and the right-hander went for it. He was too early on the shot and the ball came off the middle of the bat, but it went straight up in the air. It rose and rose and I caught sight of Matthew and Cal coming in from the left and right. Frankie too was lumbering down the pitch towards it. But it was my catch.

"Mine!" I screamed. I couldn't see whether they had stopped because my eyes were now firmly on the ball. It seemed miles away, but it was coming down faster and faster. With horror I saw it swing in the air; it was dropping in front of me. I took a step forward and thrust out my hands. There was a sharp blow on my right forearm and another on my left thigh and the ball bounced away. I'd missed it completely.

There was a shout from Frankie who was rushing back to cover the stumps. The batters had set off for a run and hesitated in the middle as they watched me bungle the catch. I saw that the ball had bounced off my leg straight into Cal's hands. He threw smartly at the stumps. Frankie, running backwards, caught it in his right hand as it flew past and threw himself at the target, demolishing all three stumps. It had all happened so fast that it was a second or two before I took it in. Then, the cheers told me that Robbie had been run out. I'd dropped Ivan Susz, the opener, and instead we'd picked up the scalp of their best batter.

"Outrageous," muttered Tylan.

"It's a privilege to be captained by such a talent," Cal said, grinning hugely at me. "To hell with the catch, he thinks, I'll kick the ball to Cal instead and we'll run out their skipper. A devilish plan."

"That's right," I chuckled.

"Do you want us all doing circus tricks? Or would you rather we took the catches and left the clever stuff to you?" Azzie asked sarcastically.

"I don't care how you get them out," I said. "Just do it."

Marty pinned Stacks Stachiewitz back on his stumps first ball and, after a moment of hesitation, Herr Dryer gave him the finger. With 23 on the board and three of their best batters back in the pavilion we had our first glimpse of the impossible.

George Kynaston and Ivan Susz set about rebuilding the innings and I sensed that Marty needed a rest. So I dropped the field out and gave Erica an over at the top end. My plan was to bring Tylan on bowling uphill into the rough and switch to the top end myself. But Erica ruined that option by throwing herself to her left to collect a stunning return catch from Kynaston from the very last ball of the over. I couldn't take her off after that. Tylan got the ball to turn sharply straightaway, so I kept the field in close, offering them the temptation of hitting him over the top. At 33 for four I needed just one more wicket before I brought back Jacky to bowl at the tail.

The score rose slowly but remorselessly. They passed the halfway mark and then the 50 came up in the twenty-second over. Erica was still bowling well and Tylan was beating the bat time and again, but with both batsmen sweeping at every opportunity, he was going for runs, too, and we couldn't afford to let them have too many. I went back to my original strategy and threw the ball to Jacky again.

"Flat out this time," I said. "I'll give you three overs to prove yourself."

Jacky pushed three balls down the leg side, which Frankie did well to stop. He was straining a bit too hard for pace – it was probably my fault for telling him to let rip. A thick edge went for three and another leg-side ball was signalled a wide by Herr Dryer, although Jacky's scowl made it pretty clear he didn't agree with him.

The final ball of the over was quick and pitched outside the off-stump. It swung in late and the batter pushed half forward and missed. It just nicked the outside of the off-stump and went through to Frankie. As the bail fell Jacky punched the air. "Five down, five to go," he said with grim determination.

They still needed 37 runs and I decided I could give Marty a little longer to rest before his final burst, so I returned at the canal end for my second spell. Cameron Armstrong chanced his arm against me and top edged a four behind the keeper.

Another lucky edge and a pull for two – this time off Jacky – took the score to 69. By now even Cal was biting his nails.

"When are you bringing Marty back?" he asked me.

"I'll give Jacky one more over, then switch him to my end," I said.

"We can win this you know."

"We're gonna win it. No question."

I ran in and bowled to Susz. He dropped the ball down in front of him and set off for a single. I picked up on the run as I continued my follow through and heard a sudden shout of "No!" from the non-striker. Alongside me the batsman struggled to turn and scramble back. I sighted the target, drew my arm back and threw – arm straight, head still – and then dived forward to give the throw extra power. The ball splattered the stumps with the batter still reaching for the line. "Out," cried Frankie. "I mean, howzat!" Herr Dryer at square-leg nearly smiled as he raised his finger.

Slim Squirrell hoiked Jacky for a cow-corner boundary and then swung again and missed. The ball hit him halfway up the front pad. It looked straight and the whole team appealed. Herr Dryer didn't even appear to think about it – his finger pointed down the pitch at the batter. 74 for seven. But now they needed only 18.

I bowled a maiden and came off. It was time for Marty. He took the ball again at the top end, though this time he was bowling to a more defensive field. We couldn't afford a slip and silly mid-off at this stage but six players were still roughly in the ring around the bat, saving the one.

The crowd, led on by the OBA, began to clap in rhythm as Mart prepared to race in. The noise grew louder and louder and there was a final cheer as the bowler's arm came over. It was quick, too quick for Cameron Armstrong, but he gloved it past Frankie for two. The next was a yorker and the batter dug it out just in time. The third was snicked down to Jacky at third-man. Marty looked furious but he responded with another yorker to Si Bannerjee; it swung into him, passed the groping bat, and the leg stump went over like a falling tree. Magic!

Dean Caroota didn't swagger out to the wicket in his usual way. The scoreboard read 80 for eight. Just 12 runs were needed for victory, but that must have seemed like Mount Everest to Deano. We needed two wickets. For the first time in the game, the odds had probably swung our way. Anything could happen now.

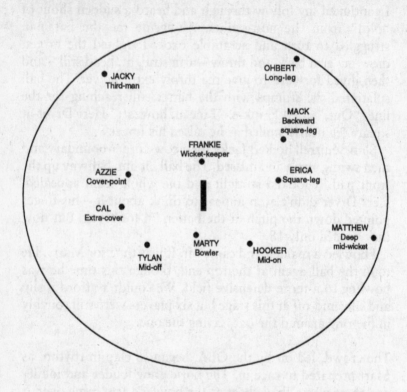

Caroota heaved and edged wide of cover point. Mack chased after it but even he couldn't stop them taking two runs. The over ended. Woolagong now needed just ten. That dropped to nine and then seven in Jacky's next over, and it was now the Woolagong players who started to get behind Deano and Cameron Armstrong. Every ball that hit the bat was applauded, every run was greeted with a mighty cheer. Jacky bowled to Dean Caroota. He carved at a ball outside the off-stump and it went off the middle of the bat. Only one fielder moved – Mack at cover point. He threw himself in the air to his left and his hand shot out and met the ball in mid-air. It was incredible, an impossible catch. Deano didn't believe it, he'd already had the shot marked down for four runs. When the awful truth hit him, his shoulders slumped and he dropped his bat. "Bonzer catch, eh, Deano?" Frankie said picking up the bat and politely handing it back to the fast bowler. "That was our Aussie, mate."

Jack Grylls was the last Woolagong batter to make his way out to the middle. He had a long discussion with Cameron Armstrong and I guessed the all-rounder's plan was to try and shield the number 11 from the bowling. Cameron faced a whole over of Marty and managed to squirt the last ball to third-man for a single. By the time Ohbert had fumbled they could have easily taken two, but one run was what they were after. Armstrong scored another single in Jacky's over, leaving Jack Grylls to face two balls. Sid turned down an lbw appeal from the first and the next whizzed over the middle stump.

Cameron pushed the score up to 88 with another run in Marty's next over. But now Marty saw his chance – he had two balls at Jack Grylls. I brought in all the fielders apart from Jacky and Ohbert on the third-man and long-leg boundaries. It was a big gamble, because they now needed only a single boundary to win the game. Marty stared at Jack Grylls, fixed the stumps in his sights and hared in like a wild thing. The yorker was just wide of the off-stump and went harmlessly through to Frankie, who clapped his hands together furiously in encouragement. Marty glared at the wicket, as if he couldn't believe he'd missed.

The last ball of the over was short of a length and Jack's patience snapped. He went for glory. A fierce slog across the line was aimed over Erica at square-leg but he got a thick top edge. The ball flew in the air towards long-leg . . . towards the lonely figure of Ohbert who was casually limping in from the boundary.

"Ohbert! Stop it!" screamed Frankie.

Ohbert looked up and saw the ball for the first time. It was in the air and coming straight for him. It seemed as if he was going to duck and let it through for four. But at the last minute he stood his ground and put both hands out in front of him. The ball slammed through them and struck him a fierce blow on the side of his head.

Ohbert staggered like boxer from a thundering left cross. The ball ballooned straight up in the air. Ohbert's knees went from under him. He fought for his balance, thrust out his right arm and as the ball dropped it landed in his open hand. And there it stayed. Ohbert rolled backwards but the arm remained upright, still holding the ball.

"He's caught it. HE'S CAUGHT IT!" roared Frankie, breaking the stunned silence. Frankie and Erica were the first to reach the spot where our hero was lying but they were quickly followed by the rest of the team and the entire OBA. For a moment it looked as if Ohbert was unconscious but then he opened his eyes and said. "Oh but . . . here's the ball, Frankie. I stopped it."

"Ohbert! It was the catch of the century," said Frankie.

"Outrageous," said Tylan.

As Ohbert struggles to stay on his feet the ball dropped into his right hand

Ohbert's catch had brought Ohbert's Ashes to an incredible end. We had won by just three runs.

HOME TEAM GLORY GARDENS V WOOLAGONG	AWAY TEAM	AT WHITMART PRIORY. DATE AUG. 6TH

INNINGS OF WOOLAGONG............ TOSS WON BY W'GONG WEATHER HOT..

	BATSMAN	RUNS SCORED	HOW OUT	BOWLER	SCORE
1	D. HOLDRIGHT	2.1.4.2	ct NAZAR	LEAR	9
2	I. SUSZ	1.1.2.1.2.1.2.2.4.3.1.1.2.2	RUN	OUT	25
3	R. GONZALES	2.1.	RUN	OUT	3
4	T. STACHIEWITZ		lbw	LEAR	0
5	G. KYNASTON	1.2.1.2	c x b	DAVIES	6
6	L.H-KIRBY	1.1.2.2	bowled	GUNN	6
7	C. ARMSTRONG	4.2.1.2.1.1.1.1.1	NOT	OUT	14
8	M. SQUIRRELL	4.	lbw	GUNN	4
9	S. BANNERJEE	2	bowled	LEAR	2
10	D. CAROOTA	2.2	ct McCURDY	GUNN	4
11	J. GRYLLS		ct BENNETT	LEAR	0

FALL OF WICKETS											BYES	1.1		2	TOTAL EXTRAS	15
SCORE	17	22	23	33	55	69	74	80	85	88	L.BYES	1.1.1.1.1.1.1.1		10	TOTAL	88
BAT NO	1	3	4	5	6	2	8	9	10	11	WIDES	1.1.1		3	FOR WKTS	ALL OUT
											NO BALLS					

SCORE AT A GLANCE

BOWLING ANALYSIS ⊙ NO BALL + WIDE																
BOWLER	1	2	3	4	5	6	7	8	9	10	11	12	13	OVS	MDS	RUNS	WKT
1 M.LEAR	:2:	::	:4.	2:	::	W2	W+:	:+:	X	2W:	::	::W	11	1	23	4
2 J.GUNN	::	M	::	:2	X	:3: W+:	2: W 2	X	::	2W:		9	1	22	3
3 H.KNIGHT	M	2:	::	:2	X	::1/2	M				7	2	16	0
4 E.DAVIES	2: W	M	:4	X							3	1	6	1
5 T.VELLACOTT	+: 2.1	::	2:	2:	X						3	0	9	0
6															
7															
8															
9															

146

Chapter Sixteen

Marty had grabbed a stump and, swinging it over his head, he now raced towards the pavilion. The adrenaline was pumping and he had a wild and dangerous look in his eyes. Jacky threw an arm across his shoulders and they careered on together, the rest of us in hot pursuit.

The TV reporter stepped forward and held out his microphone. "Brilliant finish, lads. Can I ask you for just a word . . ." He was nearly knocked over by the two fast bowlers who ran straight past him, almost through him. The crowd gathered round the pavilion clapped and cheered Mart and Jacky and then the rest of us, one by one, as we filed up the steps. The last player back was Ohbert, carried and bounced, kicking and screaming, across the ground by the OBA. He got the biggest cheer of all

Kiddo came over, grinning foolishly. "I'll tell you now, kiddo, I didn't think you had a snowball's chance in hell," he said.

"Marty and Jacky were just brilliant," I gasped.

"Brilliant! And so was everyone else. It was an amazing team performance. I don't remember seeing a better game of cricket . . . ever," Kiddo enthused – I got the feeling he meant it, too. Robbie Gonzales was standing nearby and Kiddo called him over. "It takes two teams to make a match like that," he said generously. "Woolagong played some wonderful cricket."

Robbie tried to smile. "Not good enough in the end, though."

"It could easily have gone the other way," I said, trying to sound diplomatic but thinking, Thank heaven it didn't.

"We threw it away this morning, but I'm not taking anything away from Glory Gardens. You won fair and square," Robbie said. We shook hands and then suddenly there was a bit of commotion by the door of the pavilion and I saw Wally Whitman come in with someone I instantly recognised.

"My god, it's Shane!" whispered Robbie. His eyes were bulging out of his head. But he was right. Shane Warne, or his double, had just walked into the Priory pavilion. Before I had a chance to wonder what he was doing there, Wally spoke.

"Ladies and gentlemen and players, I'm sure there isn't anyone here who doesn't know the person on my left." There was a stunned silence as all eyes fell on the great leg-spinner.

"Oh but, who is it, Frankie?" I heard our hero say.

"Mr Warne is playing at the county ground tomorrow and he has kindly agreed to come here to present the prizes for the Whitmart Tournament and Ohbert's Ashes," Wally continued. "Will everyone, including the two teams, please assemble in front of the pavilion for the presentations."

Shane Warne smiled and followed Wally out to where a table had been put up. On it stood a big silver and gold cup, the Whitmart Trophy, and next to it, a small lime green box.

Wally introduced Shane Warne again, who said that he wished he'd been here all day to witness a great cricket match. Then he picked up the Whitmart Trophy and said, "Will Robbie Gonzales, the captain of Woolagong C.C., winners of the Whitmart Tournament, please come up to receive his team's trophy." Robbie, who hadn't spoken a word since he'd first set eyes on his hero, gasped but didn't move. I gave him a rough shove and he stepped hesitantly forward and then walked up and shook Shane Warne by the hand.

"It's good to know you gave the poms a hammering in the one-dayers," Shane said with a wink. "Well done, mate."

Robbie opened his mouth to say something but no words came out. Warnie gave him another pat on the back and he turned and walked back to his place with a goofy smile on his bright-red face.

"And now for the winners of today's game," continued Shane. "Would Harry Knight please step up?"

I too shook Shane Warne's hand and stood next to him while Wally opened the green box and took out something bright orange which looked like a large eggcup with a silver-foil lid on top of it. Attached to it was a big yellow label, twice as big as the eggcup itself. Shane took it from Wally and very carefully read the label. "Please keep this way up or the Ashes will fall out." Everyone laughed. "As you all know, today's game is called Ohbert's Ashes," he continued. "And I understand that Ohbert Bennett made this splendid cup. So will he please come up and help me present it."

The OBA hoisted Ohbert on their shoulders again and carried him forward to meet Shane, who with a grin handed him the trophy. "Oh . . . but, thank you," said Ohbert who was looking even stranger than usual with a big swelling next to his right ear.

"I think you're supposed to give it to Harry," said Shane in a stage whisper.

"Oh, yes. Here you are, Hooker," Ohbert said as he handed me the cup.

When the OBA's chanting had died down a bit, Shane announced the Player of the Tournament for the one-day series, and Robbie got another chance to go up and meet his hero. This time he managed a "Thanks, Shane, mate," as he received his cheque for £25. The award for the Player of the Ashes went to Jacky Gunn for his bowling in both innings and his hat trick, though Shane said it was a close call and it could easily have gone to Marty or me.

I was proudly displaying Ohbert's cup to the rest of the team when Frankie appeared with Wally. "We've got some news for Mack," said Frankie. "We know who sent those letters."

"Who?" asked Mack and Cal at the same time.

"It wasn't anyone from Woolagong, for a start," said Frankie.

Wally produced a piece of paper. "Do you recognise the writing?" he asked Mack.

"Yes, it's the same as 'Ned Kelly'. Who wrote it?"

"It was Wally's idea," continued Frankie. "He told the OBA that Ohbert was trying to decide who was his greatest fan and suggested that they all wrote to him. This was one of the letters."

"You mean one of those lunatics sent the letters to Mack."

"But why?" I asked.

"Because they wanted Ohbert to play – and the way they saw it Mack was keeping him out of the team. That first letter was to scare him off. Whoever wrote it wanted Mack to think it came from a Woolagong player."

"It worked too," said Mack thoughtfully. "That guy must be a real sicko."

"It shouldn't be too hard to find out which one of them did it," said Wally.

"I don't care," said Mack. "They're only silly young kids. The big thing is that Ohbert and I both played – and we won. I always knew that no Aussie could have written a thing like that."

As if on cue, the jazz band immediately burst into a rousing version of "Waltzing Matilda". As soon as everyone recognised the tune, Frankie stepped forward and started to sing:

> There once was a team that came here from
>   Woolagong,
> They said, "We'll win the Ashes in England, you'll
>   see."
> And they sang all about their great deeds in Woolagong
> And bowled us out for a hundred and twenty-three.
>
> Back came Glory Gardens, they hit back at
>   Woolagong.

As Hooker lashed out at the bowling with glee
Then Marty Lear and Jacky destroyed the Aussie
*   batting*
And we won the game at a quarter to three.

We won the Ashes! We won the Ashes!
We won Ohbert's Ashes by one, two, three.
And we'll sing this song till they hear us in Woolagong.
We won the Ashes by how many? THREE!

Frankie didn't have to be asked to do an encore but this time the Woolagong boys drowned him out with the real words to the song.

Later Robbie made me promise that we'd give them a return match in Australia. "We want a chance to win back Ohbert's Ashes on our own turf," he said.

"We'll be over as soon as we've got the money together," said Mack. "I can hardly wait to show Glory Gardens round the home of cricket."

"I'll have a quiet word in Wally's ear," said Frankie.

Robbie dreamily admired the Shane Warne signature on the back of his cricket bat. "I asked Warnie if he'll come and see us in Australia, and do you know what he said? He said 'I'll be there, mate'. Maybe he'll come for the next test match against Glory Gardens."

In the scorebox Jo and Sepo were chatting happily together and comparing their scorebooks.

In the nets Shane Warne was showing Si Bannerjee and Tylan how to disguise the flipper and Robbie, Mack, Frankie and I went over to watch. It was a great end to a perfect day's cricket.

AVERAGES

WHITMART TOURNAMENT

BATTING

	INNINGS	RUNS	S/R	AVERAGE
Woolagong top four				
R. Gonzales	3	99	89.2	33.0
G. Kynaston	3	73	64.4	24.3
I. Susz	3	38	60.6	12.7
D. Holdright	3	35	75.5	11.7
Glory Gardens top four				
C. Sebastien	3	79	63.0	26.3
C. da Costa	3	75	89.4	25.0
F. Allen	3	47	110.9	15.7
H. Knight	3	28	80.6	9.3

Scoring rate (S/R) is based on the average number of runs scored per 100 balls. Minimum qualification: 20 runs.

BOWLING

	OVERS	RUNS	WICKETS	E/R	AVERAGE
Woolagong top four					
S. Bannerjee	20	83	8	4.2	10.4
C. Armstrong	11	61	5	5.5	12.2
G. Kynaston	11.1	49	3	4.4	16.3
J. Grylls	18	60	2	3.3	30.0
Glory Gardens top four					
H. Knight	17	50	5	2.9	10.0
E. Davies	16	53	5	3.3	10.6
J. Gunn	15.1	58	5	3.8	11.6
C. Sebastien	17	47	4	2.7	11.8

Economy rate (E/R) is the average number of runs given away each over. Minimum qualification: 10 overs.

OHBERT'S ASHES

BATTING

	INNINGS	RUNS	S/R	AVERAGE
Woolagong top four				
I. Susz	2	69	50.3	34.5
R. Gonzales	2	45	70.0	22.5
L. H.-Kirby	2	34	64.5	17.0
D. Holdright	2	30	71.0	15.0
Glory Gardens top four				
T. McCurdy	1*	41	80.7	41.0
H. Knight	2	77	70.9	38.5
A. Nazar	2	50	88.5	25.0
M. Rose	2	37	39.6	18.5

*Mack was not out in the first innings.

Scoring rate (S/R) is based on the average number of runs scored per 100 balls.

BOWLING

	OVERS	RUNS	WICKETS	S/R	AVERAGE
Woolagong top four					
C. Armstrong	15.2	30	3	30.6	10.0
G. Kynaston	13	24	2	39.0	12.0
J. Grylls	25	51	4	37.5	12.8
S. Bannerjee	30	87	5	36.0	17.4
Glory Gardens top four					
J. Gunn	16	59	7	13.7	8.4
M. Lear	24	70	7	20.6	10.0
E. Davies	18	19	1	108.0	19.0
C. Sebastien	10	25	1	60.0	25.0

Strike rate (S/R) is the average number of balls bowled to take a wicket.

THE CRICKET PITCH

crease

At each end of the wicket the crease is marked out in white paint like this:

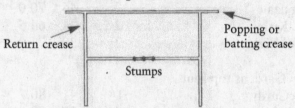

Return crease

Popping or batting crease

Stumps

The batsman is 'in his ground' when his bat or either foot are behind the batting or 'popping' crease. He can only be given out 'stumped' or 'run out' if he is outside the crease.

The bowler must not put his front foot down beyond the popping crease when he bowls. And his back foot must be inside the return crease. If he breaks these rules the umpire will call a 'no-ball'.

leg side/ off-side

The cricket pitch is divided down the middle. Everything on the side of the batsman's legs is called the 'leg side' or 'on side' and the other side is called the 'off-side'.

Remember, when a left-handed bat is batting, his legs are on the other side. So leg side and off-side switch round.

leg stump

Three stumps and two bails make up each wicket. The 'leg stump' is on the same side as the batsman's legs. Next to it is the 'middle stump' and then the 'off-stump'.

off/on side	See **leg side**
off-stump	See **leg stump**
pitch	The 'pitch' is the area between the two wickets. It is 22 yards long from wicket to wicket (although it's usually 20 yards for Under 11s and 21 yards for Under 13s). The grass on the pitch is closely mown and rolled flat. Just to make things confusing, sometimes the whole ground is called a 'cricket pitch'.
square	The area in the centre of the ground where the strips are.
strip	Another name for the pitch. They are called strips because there are several pitches side by side on the square. A different one is used for each match.
track	Another name for the pitch or strip.
wicket	'Wicket' means two things, so it can sometimes confuse people. 1 The stumps and bails at each end of the pitch. The batsman defends his wicket. 2 The pitch itself. So you can talk about a hard wicket or a turning wicket (if it's taking spin).

BATTING

attacking strokes	The 'attacking strokes' in cricket all have names. There are forward strokes (played off the front foot) and backward strokes (played

off the front foot). The drawing shows where the different strokes are played around the wicket.

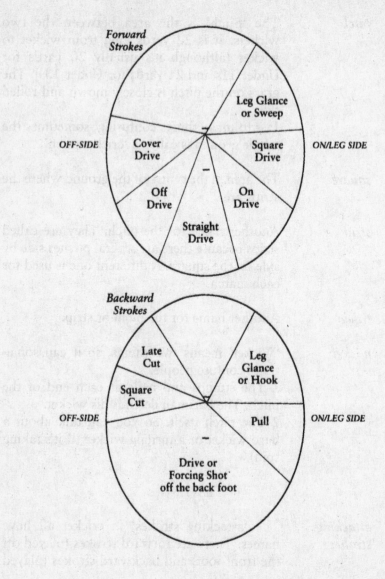

Forward Strokes

OFF-SIDE — ON/LEG SIDE

- Leg Glance or Sweep
- Square Drive
- Cover Drive
- On Drive
- Off Drive
- Straight Drive

Backward Strokes

OFF-SIDE — ON/LEG SIDE

- Late Cut
- Leg Glance or Hook
- Square Cut
- Pull
- Drive or Forcing Shot off the back foot

backing up	As the bowler bowls, the non-striking batsman should start moving down the wicket to be ready to run a quick single. This is called 'backing up'.
bye	If the ball goes past the bat and the keeper misses it, the batsmen can run a 'bye'. If it hits the batsman's pad or any part of his body (apart from his glove), the run is called a 'leg-bye'. Byes and leg-byes are put in the 'Extras' column in the scorebook. They are not credited to the batsman or scored against the bowler's analysis.
	This is how an umpire will signal a bye and leg-bye.

Bye

Leg-bye

cart   To hit a ball a very long way.

centre   See **guard**

cow shot   When the batsman swings across the line of a delivery, aiming towards mid-wicket, it is often called a 'cow shot'.

cross bat   A shot made with the bat not straight – as in the cow shot.

defensive strokes There are basically two defensive shots: the 'forward defensive', played off the front foot and the 'backward defensive' played off the back foot.

duck   When a batsman is out before scoring any runs it's called a 'duck'. If he's out first ball for nought it's a 'golden duck'.

gate   If a batsman is bowled after the ball has passed between his bat and pads it is sometimes described as being bowled 'through the gate'.

guard   When you go in to bat the first thing you do is 'take your guard'. You hold your bat sideways in front of the stumps and ask the umpire to give you a 'guard'. He'll show you which way to move the bat until it's in the right position. The usual guards are 'leg stump' (sometimes called 'one leg'); 'middle and leg' ('two leg') and 'centre' or 'middle'.

 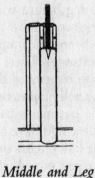 

Centre   *Middle and Leg*   *Leg*

handled the ball	Deliberate handling of the ball while in play is one of the 10 ways of being given out.
hit the ball twice	Another strange reason for dismissal. You can use your bat to stop the ball running on to the stumps after you've played a shot, but you must not strike the ball a second time to score runs or impede the fielders.
hit wicket	If the batsman knocks off a bail with his bat or any part of his body when the ball is in play, he is out 'hit wicket'.
innings	This means a batsman's stay at the wicket. 'It was the best *innings* I'd seen Azzie play.' But it can also mean the batting score of the whole team. 'In their first *innings* England scored 360.'
king pair	If a batter is out first ball in both innings he is said to have a 'king pair'.
knock	Another word for a batsman's innings.

lbw	Means leg before wicket. In fact a batsman can be given out lbw if the ball hits any part of his body and the umpire thinks it would have hit the stumps. There are two important extra things to remember about lbw: 1 If the ball pitches outside the leg stump and hits the batsman's pads it's not out – even if the ball would have hit the stumps. 2 If the ball pitches outside the off-stump and hits the pad outside the line, it's not out if the batsman is playing a shot. If he's not playing a shot he can still be given out.
leg-bye	See **bye**
middle/ *middle and leg*	See **guard**
out	There are six common ways of a batsman being given 'out' in cricket: bowled, caught, lbw, hit wicket, run out and stumped. Then there are a few rare ones like handled the ball and hit the ball twice. When the fielding side thinks the batsman is out they must appeal (usually a shout of 'Howzat'). If the umpire considers the batsman is out, he will signal 'out' like this:

| *play* | You 'play forward' by moving your front foot |
| *forward/back* | down the wicket towards the bowler as you |

play
forward/back   You 'play forward' by moving your front foot down the wicket towards the bowler as you play the ball. You 'play back' by putting your weight on the back foot and leaning towards the stumps.

You play forward to well-pitched-up bowling and back to short-pitched bowling.

rabbit   Poor or tail-end batsman.

run   A 'run' is scored when the batsman hits the ball and runs the length of the pitch. If he fails to reach the popping crease before the ball is thrown in and the bails are taken off, he is 'run out'. Four runs are scored when the ball is hit across the boundary. Six runs are scored when it crosses the boundary without bouncing. This is how the umpire signals 'four':

This is how the umpire signals 'six':

If the batsman does not put his bat down inside the popping crease at the end of a run before setting off on another run, the umpire will signal 'one short' like this.

A run is then deducted from the total by the scorer.

stance   The 'stance' is the way a batsman stands and holds his bat when he is waiting to receive a delivery. There are many different types of stance. For instance, side on, with the

162

shoulder pointing down the wicket; square on, with the body turned towards the bowler; bat raised, and so on.

striker   The batsman who is receiving the bowling. The batsman at the other end is called the non-striker.

stumped   If you play and miss and the wicket-keeper knocks a bail off with the ball in his hands, you will be out 'stumped' if you are out of your crease.

timed out   A batter will be given out if he deliberately or wilfully takes more than two minutes to come in from the moment the wicket falls.

ton   A century. One hundred runs scored by a batsman.

BOWLING

arm ball   A variation by the off-spinner (or left-arm spinner) which swings in the air in the opposite direction to the normal spin, i.e. away from the right-handed batsman in the case of the off-spinner.

beamer   See **full toss**.

block hole   A ball bowled at yorker length is said to pitch in the 'block hole' – i.e. the place where the batsman marks his guard and rests his bat on the ground when receiving.

bouncer   The bowler pitches the ball very short and

bowls it hard into the ground to get extra bounce and surprise the batsman. The ball will often reach the batsman at shoulder height or above. But you have to be a fast bowler to bowl a good bouncer. A slow bouncer is often called a 'long hop' and is easy to pull or cut for four.

chinaman A left-arm bowler who bowls with the normal leg-break action will deliver an off-break to the right-handed batsman. This is often called a 'chinaman'.

dead ball The ball ceases to be dead from the moment the bowler starts his run. However if the bowler fails to deliver the ball, the umpire will signal 'dead ball'. After the ball has been bowled it becomes dead again when it is back in the hands of the bowler or the keeper or has crossed the boundary.

donkey drop A ball bowled very high in the air.

dot ball A ball from which the batsman does not score a run. It is called this because it goes down as a dot in the scorebook.

flipper A variation on the leg break. It is bowled from beneath the wrist, squeezed out of the fingers, and it skids off the pitch and goes straight through. It shouldn't be attempted by young cricketers because it puts a lot of strain on the wrist and arm ligaments.

full toss A ball which doesn't bounce before reaching the batsman is a 'full toss'. Normally it's easy to score off a full toss, so it's considered a bad ball. A high full toss from a fast bowler is called a 'beamer'. It is very dangerous and should never be bowled deliberately.

googly

A 'googly' is an off-break bowled with a leg-break action (see **leg break**) out of the back of the hand like this.

grubber

A ball which hardly bounces – it pitches and shoots through very low, usually after hitting a bump or crack in the pitch. Sometimes also called a shooter.

hat trick

Three wickets from three consecutive balls by one bowler. They don't have to be in the same over i.e. two wickets from the last two balls of one over and one from the first of the next.

half-volley

See **length**

leg break/ off-break

The 'leg break' is a delivery from a spinner which turns from leg to off. An 'off-break' turns from off to leg.
That's easy to remember when it's a right-hand bowler bowling to a right-hand batsman. But when a right-arm, off-break bowler

bowls to a left-handed bat he is bowling leg-breaks. And a left-hander bowling with an off-break action bowls leg breaks to a right-hander. It takes some working out – but the drawing helps.

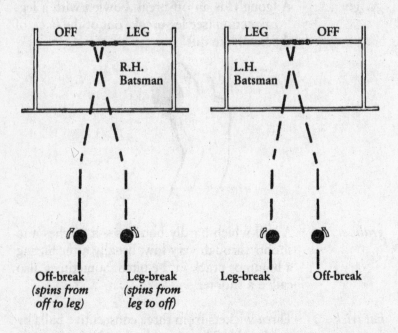

OFF	LEG		LEG	OFF
	R.H. Batsman		L.H. Batsman	

Off-break *(spins from off to leg)*   Leg-break *(spins from leg to off)*   Leg-break   Off-break

leg-cutter/
off-cutter   A ball which cuts away off the pitch from leg to off is a 'leg-cutter'. The 'off-cutter' goes from off to leg. Both these deliveries are bowled by fast or medium-pace bowlers. See **seam bowling**.

leggie   Slang for a leg-spin bowler.

length   You talk about the 'length' or 'pitch' of a ball bowled. A good-length ball is one that makes the batsman unsure whether to play back or forward. A short-of-a-length ball pitches slightly closer to the bowler than a good length. A very short-pitched ball is called a 'long hop'. A 'half-volley' is an over-pitched ball which bounces just in front of the batsman and is easy to drive.

long hop   A ball which pitches very short. See **length**.

maiden over   If a bowler bowls an over without a single run being scored off the bat, it's called a 'maiden over'. It's still a maiden if there are byes or leg-byes but not if the bowler gives away a wide.

no-ball   'No-ball' can be called for many reasons.
1 The most common is when the bowler's front foot goes over the popping crease at the moment of delivery. It is also a no-ball if he steps on or outside the return crease. See **crease**.
2 If the bowler throws the ball instead of bowling it. If the arm is straightened during the bowling action it is a throw.
3 If the bowler changes from bowling over the wicket to round the wicket (or vice-versa) without telling the umpire.
4 If there are more than two fielders behind square on the leg side. (There are other fielding regulations with the limited overs game. For instance, the number of players who have to be within the circle.)
A batsman can't be out off a no-ball, except run out. A penalty of one run (an experiment of two runs is being tried in county cricket) is added to the score and an extra ball must be bowled in the over. The umpire shouts

'no-ball' and signals like this:

over the wicket	If a right-arm bowler delivers the ball from the right of the stumps (as seen by the batsman) i.e. with his bowling arm closest to the stumps, then he is bowling 'over the wicket'. If he bowls from the other side of the stumps, he is bowling 'round the wicket'.
pace	The 'pace' of the ball is the speed it is bowled at. A fast or pace bowler like Darren Gough can bowl at speeds of up to 90 miles an hour. The different speeds of bowlers range from fast through medium to slow with in-between speeds like fast-medium and medium-fast (fast-medium is the faster).
pitch	See **length**.
round the wicket	See **over the wicket**.
seam	The 'seam' is the sewn, raised ridge which runs round a cricket ball.

seam bowling Bowling – usually medium to fast – where the ball cuts into or away from the batsman off the seam.

shooter See **grubber**.

spell A 'spell' of bowling is the number of overs bowled in succession by a bowler. So if a bowler bowls six overs before being replaced by another bowler, he has bowled a spell of six overs.

swing bowling A cricket ball can be bowled to swing through the air. It has to be bowled in a particular way to achieve this and one side of the ball must be polished and shiny, which is why you always see fast bowlers shining the ball. An 'in-swinger' swings into the batsman's legs from the off-side. An 'out-swinger' swings away towards the slips.

trundler A steady, medium-pace bowler who is not particularly good.

turn Another word for spin. You can say 'the ball turned a long way' or 'it spun a long way'.

wicket maiden An over when no run is scored off the bat and the bowler takes one wicket or more.

wide If the ball is bowled too far down the leg side or the off-side for the batsman to reach (usually the edge of the return crease is the line umpires look for) it is called a 'wide'. One run is added to the score and an extra ball is bowled in the over.

In limited overs cricket, wides are given for balls closer to the stumps – any ball bowled down the leg side risks being called a wide in this sort of 'one-day' cricket.

This is how an umpire signals a wide.

yorker
A ball, usually a fast one, bowled to bounce precisely under the batsman's bat. The most dangerous yorker is fired in fast towards the batsman's legs to hit leg stump.

FIELDING

backing up
A fielder backs up a throw to the wicket-keeper or bowler by making sure it doesn't go for overthrows. So when a throw comes in to the keeper, a fielder is positioned behind him to cover him if he misses it. Not to be confused with a batsman backing up.

chance
A catchable ball. So to miss a 'chance' is the same as to drop a catch.

close/deep
Fielders are either placed 'close' to the wicket (near the batsman) or in the 'deep' or 'outfield' (near the boundary).

cow corner   The area between the deep mid-wicket and long-on boundaries where a cow shot is hit to.

dolly   An easy catch.

hole-out   A slang expression for a batsman being caught. 'He holed out at mid-on.'

overthrow   If the ball is thrown to the keeper or the bowler's end and is misfielded allowing the batsmen to take extra runs, these are called 'overthrows'.

silly   A fielding position very close to the batsman and in front of the wicket e.g. silly mid-on.

sledging   Using abusive language and swearing at a batsman to put him off. A slang expression – first used in Australia.

square   Fielders 'square' of the wicket are on a line with the batsman on either side of the wicket. If they are fielding further back from this line, they are 'behind square' or 'backward of square'; if they are fielding in front of the line i.e. closer to the bowler, they are 'in front of square' or 'forward of square'.

standing up/ standing back   The wicket-keeper 'stands up' to the stumps for slow bowlers. This means he takes his position immediately behind the stumps. For fast bowlers he stands well back – often several yards away for very quick bowlers. He may either stand up or back for medium-pace bowlers.

colts   County colts teams are selected from the best
                 young cricketers in the county at all ages from
                 Under 11 to Under 17. Junior league cricket is
                 usually run by the County Colts Association.

under 11s/   You qualify for an Under 11 team if you are
12s etc.   11 or under on September 1st prior to the
                 cricket season. So if you're 12, but you were
                 11 on September 1st last year, you can play for
                 the Under 11s.

FIELDING POSITIONS

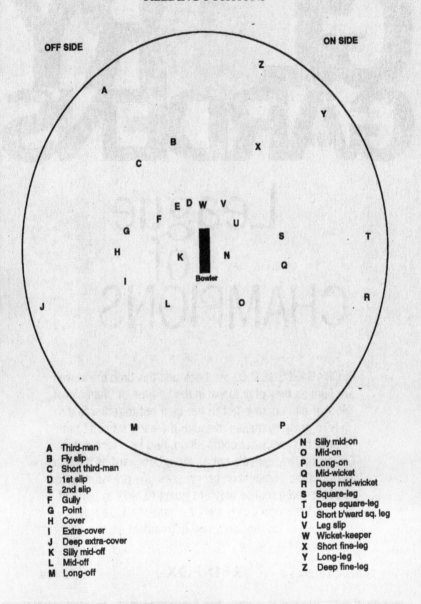

OFF SIDE   **ON SIDE**

Bowler

A Third-man	**N** Silly mid-on
B Fly slip	**O** Mid-on
C Short third-man	**P** Long-on
D 1st slip	**Q** Mid-wicket
E 2nd slip	**R** Deep mid-wicket
F Gully	**S** Square-leg
G Point	**T** Deep square-leg
H Cover	**U** Short b'ward sq. leg
I Extra-cover	**V** Leg slip
J Deep extra-cover	**W** Wicket-keeper
K Silly mid-off	**X** Short fine-leg
L Mid-off	**Y** Long-leg
M Long-off	**Z** Deep fine-leg

GLORY GARDENS

League of CHAMPIONS

GLORY GARDENS C.C. are back and this time the stakes
are high as they play to win in the League of Champions!
Hooker and co have got to get their act together fast if
they're going to make it through the early rounds to the
final of the knock-out competition. And let's face it, with
Ohbert on the team it's not as straightforward as it might
seem. As the competition progresses, the pressure builds
and the team realise they are going to have to pull out
all the stops if they want to make it all the way
to the top... and Edgbaston!

ISBN 0-09-972401-4   **RED FOX**   £ 4.99

You'll be stumped without them!